Vow

of

Solitude

By

Austen Thorne

Triplicity Publishing

2013

Vow of Solitude © 2013 Austen Thorne

Triplicity Publishing, LLC

ISBN-13: 978-0988619630

ISBN-10: 0988619636

This is a work of fiction. Names, characters, places, and incidents are the product of the author's imagination and are used fictitiously. Any resemblance to actual persons, living or dead, business establishments, events, or locales is entirely coincidental.

Printed in the United States of America
First Edition – 2013

Cover Design: Triplicity Publishing, LLC
Interior Design: Triplicity Publishing, LLC

Acknowledgements

Special thanks to Lee Fitzsimmons for spending countless hours correcting my mistakes.

Dedication

This book is dedicated to my family. Thanks for
encouraging me to write my stories.

CHAPTER ONE

Jordan walked up under the yellow tape at the scene hoping her mind wasn't telling her the truth. She looked at the beaten girl lying on the sandy bank wrapped in a bloody, white bed sheet. The body was spotted by a tourist at Land's End floating face down along the Pacific Ocean. Her name was Darcy Walker. She had been missing for two months according to the first officer and the reporter that was somehow paged to the scene. This young woman appeared to be the third victim of a serial murderer. The case had been handed to Lieutenant Detective Jordan Denali and her new partner, Rookie Detective Lance Williams three weeks prior when the first body was found.

Every one of the women were dumped in the water leading it to be found somewhere down stream. All of them blond haired, beautiful pale skinned women, brutally attacked, raped, assaulted, and then covered by only a white bed sheet soaked in each victim's blood. They all had the same beating wounds in approximately the same places, one small caliber gunshot wound to the head post mortem, as well as his signature slash mark across the abdomen. The only mark separating these bodies, his artwork, short shallow slices along the breast for the number of the girl. Jordan knew this was going to be tough.

After the body was taken away Jordan walked the

sandy beach for hours on end searching for some truth behind these mysteries. Some sort of relevance to rumors that would begin infiltrating the cover of tomorrow morning's San Francisco Examiner.

~

"Jordan, you know this is yours, you were assigned originally because of the brutal murder of the first victim. Now, with the case taking a potential turn towards a serial killer you know I would only want my best and most trustworthy handling it. The Press is going to drag it and us through the mud. I expect you to keep them informed on as little information as you possibly can. This son of a bitch has to be stopped. You know this is the kind of thing that can make or break a person's career."

"Yes sir, Captain Osborne. I understand what you're saying. I'm the highest ranking detective in our division. I'm thirty-three years old and I'm the only one on this police force with over eight years of investigation under my belt, I don't think that alone qualifies me as a veteran. Maybe it does to the rookies and the guys that stay in here and hold their desks together, I'm not saying I can't do this..."

"Don't give me that shit, Denali. You have your orders. You can and you will do this. If you decide not to...well, I can assure you it won't matter how many years you have under your belt!" The short and stocky bald man's palms were smashed flat against the top of his metal desk causing his fingers to look like sausages.

"You better get your ass out of here. You don't have long before this clown strikes again."

2

Jordan sat there for only a second hoping she could hold her tongue long enough to get back to her own office. "Look, for some unknown reason you have thrown this case at me and on top of it you're making me baby sit some desk rookie. This is bullshit, Captain. You and I both know it is." She had meant every word of it, she just didn't mean for it to come out. *Damn it Jordan, damn it, damn it, damn it!*

"Lieutenant Denali, unless you would like me to ask for your badge and weapon right now, you will march your ass out of here and follow your orders."

Jordan quickly excused herself, thanking god that she still had a job when she stepped out of the square office. *God help you, Jordan, if you fuck this up.*

~

Jordan took an elevator ride to the Medical Examiner's office to examine the bodies one more time. Maybe there was a clue, something new on the last body, something the other two bodies didn't have. As she entered the cold, well lit room, after being escorted in by a young male med student, she saw them. All three women were lined up like he would want them to look. This maniac's artwork lying one, two, three on cold metal tables each covered by a thin medical sheet, staring at her behind their closed eye lids.

How sick. She thought as her body winced along with her mind. Just then, the door opened at the other end of the room. A lean, tan woman with long dark wavy hair just past her shoulders strode in like she owned the place. She stood roughly the same height as the detective, who was standing as straight as she could to reach five seven.

Her eyes were emerald green, yet clear like shallow reef waters in the Islands. Jordan stood her ground not saying a word, only watching this figure standing in front of her. Her lips, wet and thin, but still full for kissing, moved up and down in conversation.

"I'm sorry did you say something?" Jordan could barely mumble. She was frozen, lost in admiration of this beautiful dark-haired woman.

"Yeah? What are you doing in here? Who let you in? Who are you?" the woman said before looking more closely. "Detective, I didn't notice the badge when I came in sorry. Hi, I'm Dr. Callie Marceau. I'm the medical examiner in charge of these ladies. What can I do for you? Or should I say, where shall we get started? You seem to be in your own little world." The corners of her mouth turned up to form a slight smile. "Maybe I should leave you alone for a minute. I must have walked in on you paying your respects, excuse me, I'm very sorry."

"Wait," Jordan said stepping around the table. "I'm Detective Jordan Denali. I don't think we've met," Jordan said extending her hand.

Callie couldn't help feeling a strong sudden attraction to the detective when she entered the room and saw her standing over the uncovered bodies. Jordan stood poised in black trousers, light blue button down silk blouse, matching black suit jacket and black leather shoes. Her badge flapped over her outside breast pocket of the coat. Jordan's shirt brought out her arousing, deep, ocean blue eyes. Her hair was short, almost masculine, yet fashionably feminine and very light brown, almost light enough to be called blond. She looked stiff and sharp, definitely professional, by the book, and seriously immersed in thought, not something Callie enjoyed. She preferred the wild mysterious side, never a strict rule or chapter in the book finished exactly as it was supposed to be written. One thing was for certain, Callie had never seen the detective before now.

"No, we haven't met. I'm Dr. Callie Marceau."

"I'm used to seeing Harvey."

"He's stepped into more of a management role since he was made Chief Medical Examiner for the city," Callie said. "This is my case."

Callie had just been appointed Head Medical Examiner on this case by her new boss and longtime friend, Chief Medical Examiner Dr. Harvey McCormick. She was the best of the best, she knew it, and played that card as often as need be to get what she wanted.

"I suppose you know all of the hard facts, so far?" Callie asked.

"Yes, Dr. Marceau."

"Callie. Please call me Callie. Dr. Marceau is so formal. You've known me for ten minutes so we're practically pals," Callie said with a smile.

"Okay, Callie, as you wish. They were all shot with a twenty-five caliber pistol point blank to the head and definitely post-mortem. They all have a mark on the right breast numbering them victims one, two, and three and they have a single deep laceration clearly across the abdomen, as well as being severely beaten, which is their cause of death. They were also raped post-mortem, possibly before they were shot. Have I missed anything, Doctor?"

Of course she knew she hadn't missed anything. Homicide investigation was her life and had been for over eight years. She was at the top of her graduating class and first of her class to enter the ranks of detective.

As well as, fastest rookie to ever make it to Lieutenant, not to mention top female sharp shooter for the entire state.

Jordan had been sent home from her first career choice, the U.S. Marine Corp. The discharge came two years after she joined. She was just barely twenty when she was deployed overseas due to an Iraqi assassination attempt on a former President. She was one of the first Americans to go down when her convoy was ambushed outside of Bagdad. She was imprisoned for three weeks with an extensive gunshot wound before finding an escape for herself and the other four crew members that were with her.

After her return to the U.S. she was decorated with four medals and given an Honorable Medical Discharge. She pushed those memories as far back as her mind would let her with hopes of them never resurfacing again. The only reminders she had were a small one inch scar on her lower left abdomen from the bullet entry, and a larger three inch scar on the lower right side of her back from the bullet exit.

Jordan believed it was her job to stay tightly wound, in control a hundred percent of the time. She always pushed herself past the limit like she was standing back watching someone else control her body and mind frame.

"Well, no, I don't think you've missed much in the cold hard facts department. I have some new discoveries of my own though. The bullets are all the same twenty-five caliber Smith & Wesson jacketed hollow points that are sold at every local sporting goods store within the state. As far as the gun, with no pattern to look at it's almost impossible to tell. He held the gun tight to the skin so there would be no clear powder residue marks. Now, the cuts on the abdomen were definitely made by a medical tool. A surgeon's scalpel usually makes that sort of clean cut long deep incision. Something like this one over here," she said pointing to her array of fine tools on the side table. "The number slash marks on the upper chest were also made by a medical tool, but a slightly different one. This type has a smaller blade, therefore cutting a quick short straight incision."

Jordan was impressed by the young doctor's skills. She had a strong sense of humor about her, but still professional. Jordan found that to be an attractive feature. The way she smiled at you while she spoke of her discoveries and conclusions was cocky, as if she was saying I know everything, or I dare you to prove me wrong.

Callie was capable of finding a killer in her own way using the tactical skills learned from her profession. She couldn't help having this flirty, attractive sense about her. She was strikingly beautiful and she knew it, but she didn't flaunt it.

Jordan knew it was going to be difficult speaking to this woman on a strictly professional standard. Besides, women like her were usually tied up in to some frantic relationship with a new guy every month and seeing a girl here and there on the side just for the fun of it. She would be too much to handle. *But damn she would be so worth trying to tame! Damn it Jordan, what the hell are you thinking? What has come over you? You better wake up and forget all about meeting Dr. Wild and Reckless!*

Jordan's phone rang. Shaking the thoughts from her head she answered quickly.

"Hey Jordan it's Lance, I got your message. I'll meet you at the coffee shop on Hyde and Beach. I'll take the

Trolley."

Jordan quickly said goodbye to Callie and left in a hurry.

Callie couldn't stop thinking of the blond hardheaded detective as she watched her walk away. She was strong and slightly intimidating from the shape of her legs under those pants to the way that blouse fit her perfectly showing every curve of her torso from her solid stomach line to her firm round breasts.

"She has the most piercing, passionate blue eyes I've ever seen. What the hell am I doing? I'm not a lesbian, maybe she's not either, what am I about to get myself into?" she said to the dead body on the table. She imagined the dead woman saying, 'Leave that woman alone if you know what's good for you.'

Callie laughed at herself, she knew she was going to see Jordan again eventually. What she couldn't get over was how bad she wanted to see her again.

~

Jordan and Lance walked up and down the dock at Pier 29 where the first body was found. With the current flowing in a North direction, it was obvious that she was dropped over the side of the Bay Bridge since the piers North of the Ferry Building are numbered odd and South are even. Only one pier on the North side of the Bridge is even, Pier 2.

Jordan and Lance boarded the Blue and Gold Fleet Ferry to go over to Alcatraz Island the site where the second body was found. On the Island they ran into Callie poking around away from the normalcy's of tourism that go on there. It was plain to see she was looking for the same thing and there for the same reason. *What the hell is she doing out here? What's she thinking? If she thinks she's going to start playing detective she's got another thing coming.*

Jordan's heart started to beat out of control as she introduced Lance and Callie. She looked into the wild green eyes in front of her and forgot the anger she felt when she first saw Callie standing a few feet away. She was so wrapped up in her own attraction to the doctor that she never noticed Lance's attitude take a drastic turn in favor of the beautiful woman.

"What exactly are you doing here?" Jordan asked.

"The same thing you are probably. I'm looking for something that may have been missed," Callie said. She couldn't stop thinking about the intimidating detective, she started visualizing ways to spend more time with her, possibly get closer to her. Every time Callie looked up at Jordan she saw those beautiful blue eyes staring deeply at her making her whole body shutter with excitement.

Jordan's jaw was rigid. If she could've clamped it any tighter her teeth would've broken.

"I don't need your help and I definitely don't need you traipsing all over this crime scene either."

Callie sighed. The last thing she wanted to do was get into a pissing contest with this woman. "Fine. I'll stay with you guys and traipse where you do."

Jordan shook her head walking away. Lance and Callie followed along the edge of the Island searching for answers. Any sort of clue to help them understand, maybe just maybe one small reason why, or even an insight on who was to blame for this series of cold blooded murders.

After an hour of walking around Jordan was ready to

get away from there, but did not want to leave Callie. "I'm going to call it a night. Come on, Lance, I'll let you drop me off at Hyde and take the cruiser back with you. I'll catch the trolley."

"Hey, that sounds like a plan, Jordan. I'd like to go with you if you don't mind. The trolley goes by my house as well," Callie said.

Of course, Jordan wasn't going to say no. What was another half hour going to hurt?

Callie followed Jordan into the long line waiting for the Hyde Street Trolley. Even in the beginning of June the nights were still chilly in the Bay City. The night air began to get cool after the sunset and Callie had on tight fitting low rise jeans, black leather ankle boots, and a tight white sleeveless shirt under a small form fitting leather jacket. Jordan felt her heart stop completely in the middle of a beat as the young dark-haired woman was pushed up against her side in the crowd. She felt her skin burning in every spot as their bodies touched. Her own body was sweating so intensely she could hardly move when they boarded the trolley. They both hung off the side as the cable car started its ascent up hill; Callie's long dark hair was flowing beautifully in the wind.

"Jordan, would you like to stop off with me at Washington and Jones to get a cup of lava java?"

"Interesting terms, assuming you're speaking of coffee. I think I might take you up on that offer. It would do me some good after hanging off the side of that damn thing in the cold ass wind." Her clothes were still wet from the terrible sweat that took over her body while they were in line. She was freezing in the cool night air. Luckily, Callie didn't notice the wetness on her black suit jacket.

The two of them sat inside at a small round table in the corner of the small rectangle shaped coffee house, one with a Decaf Caramel Macchiato, the other with a Mint Mocha. They discussed the events of that day. Jordan was very intuitive about whom she spoke of her cases to, very secretive. Her new partner knew very little in the case at hand. She had been stuck with him, always working as a loaner, now in charge of field training a rookie. She was designated his babysitter. She didn't like it nor did she want it to continue, he was in her way.

Callie pushed to get some kind of information out of Jordan. She couldn't help it, that was her nature. Any kind of information at all would help her, but Jordan didn't budge, not even a flinch. *She's so strong. She has this one hundred story, three foot deep, block wall around her, built so no one can enter her world. Why? There has to be a way to get Fort Knox to open up to me,* Callie thought.

As they continued their journeys home both women noticed a waded up five dollar bill on the sidewalk. Nonchalantly, they bent down at the same time to pick it up and in turn grabbed each other's hand. For one small instance Callie and Jordan locked eyes and palms. Neither woman knew what to do, Callie didn't want to let go nor did Jordan want her to. Each apologized rapidly to the other, trying to give away the bill to make up for the complete embarrassment of the whole situation. They decided neither of them needed the five dollars bad enough to attempt it again.

Callie questioned herself. *What the hell were you thinking, you're playing with fire here Case, this isn't some playful tactic to squeeze her into talking so you can get information. Where the hell are the feelings coming from? I can't control myself around her. I must be losing it.*

"Well, Doctor, this is my block here. I guess I'll see you again when I need some more of your jesting intuition." Jordan smiled as she said it, even though she didn't want to let her go on. She had to go home and go over the files again. There had to be something she was missing. Besides, that one point where she came so close to letting her guard down was enough to drive her crazy. It scared her. Jordan hadn't been in contact with this side of herself in a long time.

"Goodnight, Detective. It's been nice meeting you today," Callie said. She hated parting ways and couldn't seem to control the signals her body was setting off. She desperately hoped Jordan didn't notice the hunger burning in her eyes. Her knees were weak from the pulsating pain between her legs. Jordan's blue eyes sparkled in the moonlight. Callie wanted to feel her lips pressed against the detective's. She wanted to feel it so desperately she thought she had better turn and go before she let Jordan know that she felt that way.

All the way home she couldn't help thinking of Jordan from her slightly butch mannerisms and soldering, powerful feminine body, to the way her mouth moved when she spoke. It was always with a slight stiffness ending with one corner of her mouth turned up sort of like a quarter of a smile and one brow raised in a smirk. The lingering scent of her wouldn't go away either. Sweet yet femininely soft cologne, something she hadn't smelled before. Different from the scents she was used to. It filled the evening air, floating above her like a cloud as she walked.

~

Jordan stepped inside her two bedroom suite taking off her black suit jacket as she closed the door. She couldn't get the pressing thoughts of the young doctor out of her head. *Damn it you have to let her go, you know you can't do this Jordan, never again.* Callie had an unfamiliar wild feminine mystique about her with that dark hair and those island green eyes. Her breasts were round and perky and her butt was just as tight as the rest of her lithe body.

Jordan's mind was lost in the desire that took her over. She rushed into the cold shower noticing immediately even the cold wasn't helping. She would have to take care of this herself. She couldn't stop the aching pain between her legs any longer. She reached down frantically rubbing her swollen, hard clitoris back and forth trying so desperately to get everything about that woman out of her head. The shower stream ran down her face, between her round breasts, across her muscled abdomen, and flowed with the hot wet fluids down her thighs into the base of the tub. *Oh god, Please let her go. It has to stop. Don't do this to yourself!*

~

As usual, the alarm went off at five a.m. and Jordan headed down to the gym to begin her vigorous everyday workout of lifting weights and running on the treadmill. She finished up with ten laps around the Olympic sized pool. Then back to her suite and into the hot steamy shower.

She had a few extra minutes to eat a bagel before

grabbing her badge along with her service issued black forty-five automatic. She walked up the hill to the trolley, riding it as far as it would take her, and strode the last four blocks across to City Hall.

The San Francisco Police Departments Investigative Unit and the Medical Examiner's office were all in the same five story City Hall building. The Homicide Division took up the entire third floor and the Medical Examiner's office took up the fifth.

~

"Good morning, Lance, any new information? I see the cruiser made it back to the station safely. I'm proud," Jordan said.

"Good day to you too, Ma'am," Lance said back to her raising his voice sarcastically. "The only new information I've heard today is one of us needs to go back up to the M.E.'s office. We need the reports for the autopsy files. I will gladly go do the dirty work if you would like. I'm sure Dr. Marceau won't even be there yet. But, if she were to be there I would gladly say hello and good morning to her, from both of us of course."

"So, you think she's hot? This *is* what you're trying to tell me, right? Why didn't you just say so? Sorry to say it kid. You need to get her out of your head. That's against department policy, she's assigned to the same case. I'm sure you know the rules, rookie. Anyway, unfortunately for you, I need to go up there as well. I left one of my files in the exam room yesterday. I noticed it was missing last night when I got home. We have some other things to do first thing this morning, so we'll both go see Dr. Marceau this afternoon."

It was clear to Jordan that Lance had a thing for Callie. She tried to stop herself from being jealous. *You know she has to be into men anyway. I'll take him off this case so fast. It'll make him think twice about being straight!* She really couldn't help the way he felt though; the beautiful young doctor had sent her head into a whirlpool spin as well.

After checking with the desk Sergeant, Jordan received a small lead through the phone lines that were set up for the public to call in information. Someone had seen a suspicious car parked on the side of the Golden Gate Bridge the night before. She read the report back to Lance over and over hoping to pick up on something she could use to go on.

"Let's ride out to the South end and see if we can spot anything out of the ordinary. Also, we need to check out the odd numbered Piers. I was thinking we need to revisit the Land's End beach area as well. There could be something out there we overlooked too."

As they pulled up to the location of the third crime scene, they both noticed the woman walking around down in the sand. Callie was there searching the crime scene, following her intuition, and looking for something that had gone unnoticed. Jordan was furious. *What did this woman think she was doing snooping around her investigation?* She needed to be put in her place.

"Isn't that Dr. Marceau down there?" Lance said.

"Yeah, if you don't mind sitting here for a second I need to go take care of something." *Damn it I've had enough of this.* She left the car up in the lot and walked across the sand to where Callie was standing watching the detective as she moved closer like a hawk circling its prey.

"Well, hello there, Detective. I've been..."

"You've been snooping around sticking your nose where it doesn't belong. What the hell do you think you're doing here? This is a police investigation and a crime scene, not some mystery game for you to play with. You need to stay..." Jordan's voice had been strong and firm, Callie came right back at her with the same loud tone.

"Wait a minute, Miss, I'm in charge! I'm here doing the same thing you're doing, trying to catch this asshole, so don't come out here yelling at me because you're so pigheaded that you won't let anyone help you. You don't think I see your partner sitting up there in the car and yesterday you didn't even let him look at the files you had on the table. What kind of a partner are you? You can't push everyone away and do this on your own, Lieutenant. That's not the way it works."

"That is the way it works, besides this is none of your business. You're not an officer, nor are you a detective. You have no need to be here, your job is done. I don't want to see you around my files or my crime scenes again. I mean it, Dr. Marceau. I wouldn't want to have to go back to Chief McCormick and let him know the Assistant D.A. will be investigating one of his employees."

Callie's eyes stared daggers at her as she turned and walked away frustratingly holding back her tongue. She wanted to smack the enigmatic detective that was turning out to be a huge pain in her ass.

~

Callie wanted in on this case. And she was going to do whatever it took. She knew Jordan hadn't meant to be so vulgar, it was her nature to protect, and she was definitely protecting something. She sat at her dining table and opened up the file that just happened to end up on her autopsy table in the morgue and then into her briefcase.

In it she read Jordan's notes hoping to find something she didn't see when she read it the night before. She could hardly read Jordan's masculine chicken scratch handwriting.

Name: Lisa Griffin
Age: 25
Address: 246 Filmore Street
Hair Color: Blond
Eye Color: Brown
Height: 5'4"
Weight: 115-120
Marital Status: Married to Herbert Griffin JR. 2 yrs.
Children: None
Characteristics: Small Butterfly tattoo on lower back, shoulder length hair, small gold hoop naval ring, no visible scars or birth marks
Autopsy Record: Multiple contusions to the basilar skull, ¼ fracture on left side of skull, two one inch long ¼ inch deep incisions on right breast, 10 inch long ½ deep laceration along abdomen just above naval, twenty-five caliber shot point blank range to the right side of the skull post-mortem, forced entry and tears along vaginal walls also post-mortem
Suspects: Herbert Griffin JR.,
Crime Scene: Alcatraz Island
Notes: Autopsy completed by Dr. Callie Marceau confirms findings to be consistent to victim #1

subsequently making Griffin #2, found by tourists 3/15, 13:30 p.m. floating face down along the rocks on the North end of the island, potentially dropped off of the Bay Bridge 3/14 around 02:00a.m., found only wearing identical style white sheet as victim #1, according to Dr. Marceau, knife wounds more than likely from surgeon's scalpel set, possibly 4-6 fatal blows to the skull with large blunt object, rape, slice markings, & gunshot all post-mortem, bullet is linked to same gun, husband questioned twice - out of town on business alibi still holding firmly.

Callie knew she had to see the other files. She kept wandering what was missing. She needed to see Jordan again and the more she thought about it the more she *wanted* to see her again.

"Damn it, Callie, you're NOT a lesbian. Get over this infatuation before you get hurt!" she said to herself slamming the file closed.

The next day she called the number on the card Jordan had left her the first day she was there in case any new developments came up during the autopsies.

"This is the voicemail for Detective Denali. I'm either away from my desk or my phone is turned off. Leave a detailed message and I'll return your call. If this information is urgent please call my office at the station."

"Detective, this is Dr. Marceau. I was wondering if we could talk. I may have some information you could utilize. I'll be here in my office until four. I know I gave you my business card, but I'm calling from my cell phone so you can call this number if it's after hours."

She hated leaving messages, this would mean the detective would have to call back eventually and she would have to sit on pins and needles waiting for the call.

18

Wanting and needing to hear Jordan's husky voice was driving her senseless. She wanted Jordan's body wrapped around her, which was completely unexplainable to her, but she also wanted the cold hard facts to this case just as badly. Solving mysterious serial cases like this was in her blood. Her father had been a criminal investigator for most of his life. He passed away while working on a headliner case in 1992 when Callie was only nine years old.

CHAPTER TWO

Jordan jumped on the elevator just before the doors closed and pushed number three. She turned around to find Callie standing there by herself against the back wall in low rise black pants and a dark purple short sleeved blouse. Callie's hair was long and slightly wavy to her shoulders. She always wore it down. Her eyes seemed darker in the bright lights of the elevator. Jordan didn't know what to say to her. All she could think about was kissing her. *Jordan, you have got to get these damn thoughts out of your head. It's only going to hurt you.*

"I assume you never received my message, either that or you're ignoring me," Callie said.

"Yeah. I did get it. I just...well, I caught a break in the case and was working on it for a few days." She wanted to say she was sorry and she dialed the phone over and over and yet hung it up. She was mad, but not angry. The only way she knew how to handle this intriguing woman was to be forceful. When it came to her work, Jordan was serious about what she did and didn't appreciate people snooping around or getting in the middle of her investigations. Her cases were her life. She had to keep herself from acquiring feelings that she hadn't felt in a long time. Pushing Callie away made things somewhat easier. No one had ever been able to break Jordan, but the young doctor was heading slowly down the right path.

"I hope it was a decent size break. My information turned out to be something you already knew anyway. I should've known a mighty case hungry detective like you would have no problem finding the answers to all of the questions," Callie said pushing off the wall.

"How did you..."

"I talked to your partner. He let me know that you knew about the husband and he said he would take care of any new details I came up with. He also asked me to dinner. Unfortunately, I had to let him down. My desk has files stacked two feet high, which is why I'm on the way back up there. I went down to the lobby for a muffin and the damn lady was already gone. Who the hell runs a muffin stand for only an hour?" Callie said shaking her head.

"Here's my floor. I hope you get your paperwork caught up. Try the bakery down the road next time. Their muffins aren't stale. By the way, Lance knows he can't have a relationship with anyone involved in a case he is assigned to. I have already discussed this with him." Jordan couldn't stop this woman from being attracted to her rookie partner. He was definitely nice looking and physically fit, with sandy colored light brown hair and little beady-like dark eyes. He was close to Callie in age and roughly the same height as Jordan and Callie, which made him a short guy.

"Does that pertain to you too?" Jordan acted as though she never heard the seductive question .

"Have a nice day, Lieutenant," Callie said as the detective stepped out of the elevator. "What the hell are you doing? Go ahead, throw yourself at her, make her run even further. I swear you're turning out to be a lesbian after all, either that or you're coming down with something," Callie said to herself as the doors closed once again.

Jordan couldn't quite understand why Callie kept calling her, lieutenant. Yes, that was her rank but she was a detective. No one in the Homicide Division was ever called by their rank. The fact that Callie had chosen to use that as a formal way of talking to her seemed rather odd. Jordan didn't much care for it since it was a formality around the station when you needed to get someone's attention on a serious note, sort of like using military ranks.

Jordan wondered why had she been so drawn to this case. Homicide cases went through both of their desks quite often, yet they had never met until last week when both were handed this assignment. Jordan sat at her desk listening to the voicemail still left on her phone from three days before. The young doctor's voice sounded excited and nervous at the same time which was different since Callie was always so sure of herself. She wasn't too cocky, but damn sure she knew what she was doing.

~

Jordan was looking for Lance since he wasn't answering his phone. She'd been sitting at her desk going over some paperwork when she realized she forgot to ask Callie for the file she left in the exam room. They were caught up in the argument on the beach at the crime scene and after the interaction in the elevator she forgot all about the document. She realized it was missing when she opened her briefcase. Since Lance was nowhere to be found she figured it wouldn't hurt to go get it herself, even though she needed to chew his ass again for crossing the fine line between himself and the other employees on his case.

Jordan walked out of her small, almost square, corner office with dark gray walls shutting the door behind her as usual. She passed Lance's small cubical desk along the wall and stepped into the elevator she shared that morning with Callie. Her soap and light perfume scent still lingered in the air. *You have to keep it together here. Don't let your guard down, she smells fear.* The pep talks never seemed to work, yet she still insisted on using them.

When she walked out of the elevator on the fifth floor she ran into a young colleague of Dr. Marceau's. According to the ID tag clipped to the lapel of her suit jacket, her name was Chloe and she was the psychologist for the M.E.'s office. Jordan thought she was definitely cute, younger than both herself and Callie which would make her in her mid-twenties if she had to guess. She had blond hair just above her shoulders and brown eyes. Her short black skirt showed off a nice pair of lean, sun-tanned legs.

"Hi, I'm Chloe, you must be one of the detectives by the looks of your badge hanging there," Chloe said.

Callie noticed Chloe looking up and down at the figure standing in front of her as she walked up behind the detective. Jordan could feel the warmth of the body right behind her. She was almost breathing into Jordan's ear, holding the jealousy back.

"Chloe, I see you've met Detective Denali. This is..." Before she could finish her sentence Jordan stepped forward shaking Chloe's hand.

"Hello Chloe, it's nice to meet you."

Callie immediately started walking Jordan in the opposite direction to get Chloe's paws off of her. "She's our psychologist here. She talks to the family members when they come to claim the bodies. She just graduated from college and took her boards recently."

"Dr. Marceau, I left something here a few days ago. I'm here to reclaim it back if you please."

They walked down the hall to Callie's office, which was roughly the same size as Jordan's, but with a leather couch along one side. The walls were the same dull gray color. Her desk was a mess, papers going in every direction. A huge difference compared to Jordan's which was always frantically neat and profoundly organized. Her office also had the same frosted glass windows with all of the blinds open. Jordan on the other hand kept most of hers closed with only the ones either side of the door staying open. It was apparent that most of the offices were similar throughout the large building they shared.

"I know I've told you, please call me Callie. You make things out to be so formal."

"I hope you haven't opened this, it's an official police investigation file. I wouldn't want to hold you in contempt for defacing police property. Wait, what am I saying? I know you read the damn thing. I would've picked it back up a while ago, but I forgot all about it after I just so happened to run into you at Land's End," Jordan growled.

~

Callie couldn't help noticing the way the detective was standing, practically like a Marine Sergeant drilling one of her slave Private's. Callie tried to decide whether

24

to take the verbal scrutiny and let her go, or back her up against the wall and ease the pain. It was obvious that Jordan was into this case way too far. *What the hell is driving her to this? Why? On top of that, what the hell is driving me to her? I've never been this head strung over anyone before, especially a woman. I have to be losing my damn mind.*

It was hard not to notice that Jordan's suits were always neatly pressed and form fitting right to her body, sometimes Callie would catch herself staring right through the clothes, picturing the curves of nude skin underneath. This woman cared enough about presentation to make sure she looked sharp and in control every second. *How the hell can anyone resist the temptation to just pull her body up against yours, fall into those beautiful blue eyes, and take control of those soft lips? Damn it Callie, here we go again, get a grip woman!*

"Look we need to talk about this. I don't want you to hate me, I'm just trying to do my job, as I'm sure you are too," Callie said.

Jordan was about to walk out of the room when her cell phone rang. "Yes, Captain, I'll be right there." She ran down to the elevator with the Callie running after her to see what was going on. The elevator door was closing as she turned back towards Callie.

"Stay out of this, it doesn't concern you."

~

Thirty minutes later, Jordan walked out of the Captain's office with this look on her face that no one had ever seen before. Lance followed her to her office hoping she'd fill him in as she shut the door in his face. She had just been briefed on what seemed to be victim number four. This time their guy decided to take things not just out of town, but out of state, and clear across the country. *What was his plan? His game?* She was only one of the many pawns in the sick twisted game of cat and mouse. Jordan sat in the swiveling office chair behind the metal desk, her mind racing with fury. *Who are you? What do you want with me? This can't be, unless you're trying to trip me up. Damn you, why change the rules now? I will still find your ass one way or another. It doesn't matter where the fuck you are!*

~

Sitting at the airport Jordan saw Callie walk by. She quickly threw up the newspaper not realizing it was upside down.

"So, we meet again, Detective. Why are you reading...oh never mind, I'm getting use to your weirdness. Did you save me a seat on the flight or should I start running now so I can catch a ride on the wing of your bird?" She stood there with both corners of her thin full mouth pointed up, trying to hold in a laugh. The gloss shined on her lips in the bright airport lighting.

Jordan tossed the upside down newspaper aside. "No, I never said you couldn't get on my uh...bird was it that you said. It's none of my business where you fly to on your own time. Don't let me stop your vacation." Jordan wanted to reach up and pull Callie's mouth down onto hers so intensely her blood was boiling with excitement. She could hardly speak another word.

"Look, whether you like it or not, Miss Thing, I'm not going on vacation. The D.A. is serious about catching this guy, so I'm being sent to Florida with you. I noticed your crotch happy partner isn't here. I don't remember his name. I keep calling him Woody for obvious reasons, but that's neither here nor there. What seat are you in? I'm assuming we are supposed to stick together on this trip. I'm going along to take a look at the new body and match it to my notes on the other three. We're both here on business. I won't get into your way if you don't get into mine. I do have just one question for you, Lieutenant, why are you always so tight? You never let loose, not even once. Why is that? I'm sure deep down you want to be nice to me and let me do my job just as you go about doing your own. Deep down you want a partner and you know you want to work with me. We can help each other, you know that. Stop kidding yourself. I'm tired of watching you suffer," Callie said sitting beside her with a small smirk on face.

Jordan was shocked at the set of balls the young doctor had grown. Whatever crawled up her ass was not going to get in the way of what Jordan was being sent there to do. Of course, she wanted Callie with her. Not just on this case or on the job, but all the time, on duty, off duty, in her house, in her shower, lying naked with her in her bed. She wanted her and she couldn't stop thinking about it.

"Would you please stop calling me lieutenant? I'm a detective not a soldier or sailor," Jordan said. "Police ranks work a little differently in case you haven't noticed."

Callie shrugged.

~

They both boarded the plane to find they were seated together. Jordan was by the window for the long flight to Florida. Callie was happy she had a seat next to her. Now, the unfathomable detective would have to talk to her sometime during the flight. Besides that, she knew it was going to drive her mad being that close to her for that long with their arms right next to each other casually touching. Jordan's scent wouldn't go away. It seemed to be embedded in Callie's lungs as she breathed the soft fragrance mixed with soap.

She wondered what kind of mysterious past was behind Jordan's dark blue eyes. Callie was bound and determined to find out. Just as she started to speak, Jordan pulled out her laptop and began reading the document that was sent to her on the new victim. She turned the screen just a bit so the sneaky doctor couldn't read what it said.

Subject: The Bay City Killer
Date: 5/12
From: DetJ.Juarez@MDPD
To: DetJ.Denali@SFPD

Detective Juan Juarez

Name: Unknown
Age: 20-23
Hair color: Blond
Eye color: Hazel
Characteristics: Small tattoo on left shoulder, no other marks, no body jewelry
Notes: Small cut on right breast, gunshot wound to the head, severe beating in the head and cut across stomach

area, appearance of possible rape

Detective Denali this is all we have to go on so far. It appears to be the same guy but hopefully you can give some insight when you compare her to your three cases. Thanks again for your cooperation.

Detective Juan Juarez
Miami-Dade Police Department

As she finished reading the file and drawing somewhat of a similar comparison she noticed that Callie was sleeping soundly next to her, a slight smile graced her lips. Her shirt collar draped open just enough to see the never ending natural tan that extended down into her cleavage. Jordan felt an uncontrollable urge to push the dark hair back away from Callie's face. *No, you have to stop this. You can't let this girl get control of you.* She wanted so deeply to take Callie into her arms. It had been so long since she'd held another woman, almost too long to remember. Pushing away every painful detail of her past somehow helped her with the oncoming tides of the present and the future. This was who she was, a lonely, single, mysterious woman with a secluded history she swore she would never tell. She made herself out to be this way. Her heart was barely mended from a time before when she let her feelings and passions drive her innocence over the edge.

~

On the way to the hotel, Callie decided she was going to learn about these cases whether Jordan wanted her to or not. There were definitely more ways than one to get information out of a person. She couldn't get the images from the light sleep and somewhat daydream she found herself in on the plane. Jordan's muscular, tanned thighs wrapped around her body moving gently up and down as the beads of sweat ran down her sides. She couldn't quite make out where they were. It was sunny, like a beach but no scenery, and hot, so hot their bodies melted into one another. What a torrid dream she thought to herself as the memory of it still lingered on her mind. *Whoa, you need to get control of yourself damn it.*

"This is bullshit, lady. We have two separate reservations how the hell are we staying in the same room? I don't see any reasoning to this at all. Maybe if I speak Spanish you will understand. I'm not staying in the same room as Her!" Jordan raised her voice.

"Ma'am, if you would just calm down and..."

"And what, let you tell me how this is all your mistake and unfortunately you're sorry but the hotel is all booked up and there is nothing you can do."

"Look, Jordan we can work this out it's really no big deal. So what, you have to spend a few days, and now nights with me. I'm adult enough to get through this, I assume you are too," Callie said.

Jordan snatched the key cards out of the ladies hand trying not to give her the finger as she stormed off into the elevator. "What a bitch!" She growled.

She wasn't literally mad at the front desk lady, just pissed at the fact the she was stuck in the same room as Callie. Her body wanted her bad enough, now she would have to see her constantly for the next three days. She was hoping to have a room to herself to be free, to get some paperwork taken care of, or to even relieve herself if need be. At least it was a two room suite, albeit smaller than the one she was living in back in San Francisco.

"Look at this room. You were making an ass of yourself back there for nothing. We have separate bedrooms. It's not like I'm going to push my way into your bed, unless of course you want me in there." Callie's mouth spoke before she had time to edit the sentence.

Yes I want you there. Jordan thought as her body overpowered her mind.

Callie walked over by the arm of the couch the detective was sitting on, making sure to move close enough to run her thigh across Jordan's arm that was draped over the side. Jordan let her stay that way, feeling the burning fire in her arm as their bodies touched for only a second before moving her arm out from between Callie's thigh and the couch. She stood up taking her dark gray suit jacket off revealing her shoulder holster and pistol. The straps going under her shoulders and around her back pulled her shirt in tight around her breasts. She laid the jacket over the back of the chair on the opposite side of the room and turned to remove the gold badge from her coat's front pocket.

Callie noticed the black forty-five caliber automatic hand gun that was snapped tightly under Jordan's left arm. She looked intimidating and sexy standing there. Callie felt safe with her.

"Does wearing that thing strapped to you like that ever bother you? It would drive me crazy," Callie said.

Jordan turned back towards the dark haired woman. "After a while you get used to it. It sort of becomes part of you. You actually feel weird when it's not on you like you're naked or something's missing."

Callie couldn't help mumbling under her breath. "I

31

bet you don't feel weird naked." Fortunately, Jordan didn't hear her.

"Hey, which room do you want? I need to unpack and go over some of my work before we go to the morgue," Jordan said.

Callie chose the doorway on the right side of the wall leaving Jordan the balcony room. She couldn't stop thinking about the detective with the gun anchored to her body. It looked masculine on top of her femininely hard frame. Even lying loose in the room she was as sharp as a razor, never letting her guard down. It was almost like she was always expecting the worst.

Callie decided to go down to the lobby bar and have a drink while Jordan studied her notes like a college student for an exam. Noticing an entertainment bulletin board in the lobby, she walked over to see that it was full of flyers and business cards. One of them seemed to be very interesting, it read: Lipstick/Diesel, he/she, fag/drag, straight up or down, we have something for you at *All Of The Above!* She stood there reading it over and over a few times to make sure she understood it correctly.

"You ever been?" A tall dark haired man standing behind spoke with a thick Spanish accent.

"Excuse me?" She said.

"All Of The Above? You ever been there?"

"Uh...no. You?"

"I own it. I'm here picking up my friends that flew in from New York to see me. You should check it out. It's the best place in town. It doesn't matter your style, we have as it says, all of the above." He started to walk away and turned back towards her. "Out the front door, two blocks to you left, you can't miss it."

She sat down ordering a beer from the bartender and

decided she wanted to check the club out. She knew Miss Hard Ass upstairs wasn't going to go with her and probably would cause a big deal if she went alone. It was worth a try though. After finishing her beer she went back to their room.

Callie entered the suite noticing right away that Jordan was still closed up in her room. She knocked softly on the bedroom door.

The door opened and Jordan's head popped out. "Yes, can I help you? I see you didn't find someone to run off with while you were down there. Damn the bad luck," Jordan said.

"Ha-ha. You should be a fucking comedian, I'm laughing so hard on the inside I swear you should see this." Callie shook her head slightly trying to erase the thoughts of the detective creeping up in her mind.

"Are you ready to go yet?" Callie asked. "I want to get this preliminary meeting over with and maybe we can get some dinner afterwards. I was talking to someone downstairs about this place up the street. I think I may try it out tomorrow night after I catch up from the jet lag."

~

At the morgue they ran into a few blue shirt street officers standing around talking about the body. Jordan finally found Detective Juarez's office after walking down all of the hallways. It was obvious that all of the officers and detectives there were pissed that someone was called in to check out their case and a woman at that. She knocked twice on the wooden door and a tall, athletic looking, Hispanic man opened it while talking on his phone.

"Come on in." He was older than Jordan thought. His grayish colored hair gave it away. He looked surprised to see how young and beautiful the two women were.

"Hey let me call you back Gene, Detective Denali is here from California." He extended his hand towards Jordan, then looked up and down at the dark-haired woman beside her.

"Hi, I'm Juan. Everyone calls me JJ. How was the flight? Is this your partner?"

"Our flight was great," Callie said.

"No, she's our Medical Examiner for this case."

"Yes, I heard you were going to be here too, Dr. Marceau? Correct?" He said shaking her hand a little longer than normal.

Jordan rolled her eyes and followed him downstairs to the morgue. The Medical Examiner pulled a metal drawer out of the wall revealing the cold body. He pulled the thin white sheet back exposing her from the waist up. She had blond hair and a thin figure that was similar to those back in San Francisco. The autopsy had not been started yet since Dr. Marceau was there to work with the Dade County Medical Examiner in case they had a match.

The process took three hours, from start to finish. Jordan stood there in silence watching the details while the procedure was performed. A few moments into the transition Jordan lost sight of the body lying on the table. Her eyes focusing only on Callie, her small hands, the shifting of her torso, with her delicate eyes fixed solely on her work. The beautiful young doctor looked so smooth as she went through the vigorously detailed steps and stages going over this woman's body with a fine toothed comb. There was definitely a similar form in the markings on this woman. The tests results would show whether or not she was a match for their case.

~

Back at the hotel, Jordan sat in her room going over her notes from the autopsy. The test results wouldn't be ready until first thing in the morning. Callie was on the couch in the living room watching Batman on the movie channel. Never having seen it, she was following the story closely. She didn't notice Jordan walk out of her room wearing a white, tight fitting tank top showing off her round breasts tucked beneath a sports bra, dark blue warm-up pants, and sneakers on her feet.

"I'm going down to the gym. Call me if something comes up," Jordan said.

Jordan never missed a day in the gym. It always helped clear her mind of her stressful work. She worked out this time not only to help ease the pressure of the case, but to try and find some way to regain control of her mind. She couldn't make herself escape the tantalizing thoughts of Callie streaming round and round like a kaleidoscope in her head. *Please leave me alone, I don't want you, you can't make me want you. Oh god why won't you go away? Please!* No matter how hard she tried, the reflections remained.

~

Callie heard the lock snap and turned her head towards the door. Jordan was standing there soaking with sweat from head to toe. Callie felt a deep sensation between her legs while staring at Jordan's sweaty upper body. She was speechless, lost in admiration for this sexy creature she wanted to devour.

"Still watching Batman huh, I haven't seen that in years," Jordan said in Callie's direction as she walked past the television and into her room. She returned with a small stack of clothes on her way to the bathroom and quietly pulling the door closed behind herself. She peeled off her sweaty clothes and entered the steaming shower. Her body was soft and limp from her workout. She stood there feeling the water rush wildly through her short hair and down her body over and over. When the water finally became so cold she could hardly stand there, she quickly shampooed her hair and lathered the soap onto her tanned skin.

~

Jordan walked out of the bathroom wearing a pair of gray cotton sweat pants and a small white tee shirt with the Marine Corps logo on the front. She looked cute with her hair still slightly wet and not brushed. Her appearance made her look like she was in her early twenties. The detective always wore her hair in the messy, un-brushed style, sort of like she just woke up.

Batman Returns had almost finished and Batman Forever was next in line as part of the four movie series playing on TV.

"Have you really never seen these movies, Callie?" Jordan couldn't help but ask. Although, it was her favorite series of movies, she knew she wanted to watch something else tonight.

Callie couldn't stop staring across the couch at Jordan sitting there with her feet up on the table. It was all she could do not to ravish her and she had no idea how to even ravish a woman to begin with. She thought Jordan was attractive the first time she saw her, but now she looked so different, almost sweet and innocent.

Jordan felt the hair on her arms stand up and she looked over to Callie staring deeply at her. A rush of shyness ran throughout her veins. She knew that look anywhere and any other time she'd be willing to give into the temptation, but Callie wasn't some stranger in a bar that she'd never see again.

Callie took a deep breath and focused her eyes back on the TV. Her heart was racing so fast she was scared to look down in case it was thumping out of her chest like a cartoon. *Damn Callie, you just let the cat run right out of the bag and prance around the living room. What are you going to do now, huh? She's a lesbian, at least you think she is. Now, she probably assumes you're one too. Oh my god I'm a lesbian, at least I think I'm one. How the hell did this happen? I mean yeah, I've had thoughts of women, even used seductive moves on women to get information that I wanted, but this, this is so much more, and completely different. Shit! Talk about a wakeup call!*

"Would you like to order room service? I don't really feel like going out," Jordan said.

"Sure! Food, that's a good idea. I'm hungry too," Callie clamored. She couldn't help feeling a little uncomfortable and nervous. She'd just been caught in a moment she wished to forget, as well as cherish.

Jordan could hardly speak their order to the desk clerk on the phone. She wasn't sure how to take the idea of knowing Callie was into her. Part of Jordan wanted to get it all out in the open and clear the air so to speak, but she knew it was easier to just ignore it.

~

Callie wanted to know Jordan's opinions on the case. She felt like Jordan was hiding something and she was prepared to stop at almost nothing to get it. Callie enjoyed being around the detective, when she played nice. She noticed that Jordan was capable of being a sweet, almost innocent human being at least once during their trip. They ate their dinner and continued watching the movie series.

Jordan kept looking over at the doctor out of the corner of her eye. The temptation was growing rapidly between them. Callie couldn't help sending signals to Jordan. Her body did it without warning. Neither woman would succumb to the pressure as they went separately to their rooms, both wanting the other, yet knowing it was best to push aside those lascivious feelings.

Jordan refused to let herself dream, yet every time she closed her eyes she saw the face of the woman in the room next to hers. Callie begged herself to let go of the feelings she could no longer control. *Damn it I've never dealt with this before, what's wrong with me, what are you doing to me Jordan?*

CHAPTER THREE

"Good morning, Detective, Doctor. I hope you ladies are enjoying your stay here. I'm sure you would like to take your rental car to the crime scene." Detective Juarez said.

"Yes, that would be great." Jordan cut him off. Of course she wanted to take her own car. She wasn't dependent upon anyone.

They arrived at the East end of the bridge presumed to be the place the body was dumped. About a quarter of a nautical mile downstream was where she had been found by two fishermen. The woman was seen floating face down in a white sheet covered in blood. Jordan and Callie both examined the area and studied the location while frantically writing notes. Jordan found herself too caught up in her crime scene investigation to notice the Miami-Dade detectives and officers milling about and staring at the gorgeous, dark-haired beauty next to her.

"Were there any witnesses, Detective Juarez? Anyone see a suspicious car around, anything like that, tire tracks, foot prints?" Jordan was hoping for something to support her intuition, given the lack of information from the crime scene she almost expected this investigation to come up short.

"Well, Detective Denali, my guys searched here forty eight hours straight and they're actually still out here searching. No one has really come up with anything concrete. No witnesses. Just a body and the fishermen who found her. Both men have been questioned and aren't linked at all to the young lady. I wish I could give you more to go on. Unfortunately, this is all I have," Juan said. He wanted this to be the Bay City Killer and out of his jurisdiction. Miami had enough crime, rape, and murder, but never anything like this. This was serious, too serious for his team and he knew it.

Back at the M.E.'s office Jordan carefully listened as Callie went over the examination results. She tried to focus on the matter at hand instead of the dark-haired doctor and the tight low cut shirt she was wearing.

As Callie started talking she took a quick glance around the table at everyone standing in front of her. She locked eyes with Jordan for what seemed like minutes, but were actually only mere seconds. Those mysterious deep blue eyes were affixed solely onto hers. This brought a tiny smile to her face.

"Where to begin...well guys, we've concluded we don't have a conceivable match. This woman's marks are similar yes, but identical, no. The bullet is not a match to the ones we have and the sheet fibers are not a match either. Looking closely at her lacerations, to the naked eye they're smooth and texture free, under the microscope they have jagged edges meaning this was probably a fairly new pocket knife style blade. Also, this woman's hair has been recently colored blond. Probably after he killed her. There are no follicles on her scalp that show excessive coloring or bleaching. Her natural color is almost as dark as mine, meaning she would have to dye her hair monthly to keep it looking this natural."

"I agree with you, Doctor," Jordan said. "Frankly, this means you guys have a copycat on your hands. It's actually good news for both of us. You have a loser playing media games and we still have our killer back at home instead of parading all over the country." Jordan relaxed briefly, but it never showed on her face.

"Thank you, Detective Denali, and a huge thanks to you, Dr. Marceau. You two make a great team." Detective Juarez said.

Callie looked up to find Jordan looking directly at her. She could feel the pressure of those deep blue eyes piercing through her. *My god she's going to drive me crazy looking at me like that. I don't know how much I can take. I want to jump into those puddles of ocean and swim for days. Callie, chill out girl before you let on to the rest of the group that you're head over heels for this woman.*

~

Jordan made the decision not to fly back until the next morning since it was already late in the afternoon and their hotel and flight plans were arranged for the next day anyway. Callie was happy because she wanted to check out that bar down the street.

Back at the hotel Jordan quickly called the station to let the captain know it wasn't the same person and they would be home the following day. The captain had kept Lance in San Francisco in case the killer decided to strike there again during the time Jordan was gone. After she hung up her cell phone she proceeded to type all of her hand written notes into the case file on her computer.

Callie stretched out on the couch like a lazy cat and turned the TV on instead of watching Batman two nights in a row. She was in fact watching the elusive detective sitting there at the small desk typing away on her laptop, her leather holster still strapped around her shoulders with the gun behind her back firmly in its case. The back of her baby blue colored blouse had wet spots in the center where she had been sweating from wearing her suit jacket. June in Miami was completely opposite of June in San Francisco. The Florida heat and humidity was killing both of them.

"Are you able to go without TV?" Jordan hissed as she continued to type.

"Well, yeah, I'm bored. What would you like me to do? You won't talk to me about your case," Callie scowled back at her. *I wish you would talk to me about anything. The weather, the carpet, your feelings, your past. Anything!*

"I didn't think you would be into boxing. You look more like you're into Soap Operas."

Callie felt like smacking her in the back of the head. *What a pain in the ass.* "Yeah, kiss my ass." She said laughing. Jordan cracked a smile as well.

"Hey, I'm thinking of going to that bar I told you about last night. Would you be interested in going, or are you too wrapped up in official detective bullshit to go have a drink?" She couldn't believe she was able to get the words out. It wasn't a date but sounded like a date or a semi-date or something to that sort.

Jordan was a bit shocked at first. "I really can't...I shouldn't. You can go. I'm not your baby sitter." She wanted to go along terribly, but fraternizing was against the rules in her world.

"Look if you want to sit here with your laptop up your ass that's fine with me. I'm going to go have a drink. It's two blocks down on the left, if you change your

mind,"
Callie said going into her room.

Callie came out a few minutes later wearing black hip hugger pants that wrapped around her lean, well-toned legs and a tight black low cut top that showed her tan stomach just barely if she moved a certain way. She zipped up her black leather ankle boots and walked over to Jordan, who was sitting at the desk watching her out of the corner of her eye. The dark haired woman bent down next to the detective's cheek not even looking at the screen in front of her that she had been dying to read.

"Chicken," she whispered into Jordan's ear softly, her lips barely brushed against the tender skin of the other woman. She walked out the door without looking back.

Jordan scowled and was pissed that Callie had just done that to her. She was turned on by the way the young doctor was dressed, but now her body was aching for pleasure after that little stunt. She could still feel her breathing on her neck and into her ear. "What a bitch!" Jordan said tossing a couch pillow at the closed door.

An hour later Callie was sitting at the bar in the Lesbian room contemplating dancing with the masculine figure sitting next to her. She'd been in places like this before and played the role quite well when it came down to getting some bit of information on a case she was interested in. She just never actually thought of going home with one of the women or falling for another woman for that matter. Out of the corner of her eye she thought she saw the stubborn detective, but then turned away. *There's no way she would come here. She's too stiff, especially for this room.*

Callie was startled when the hair on her arms stood up. It was hot as hell in there and she wasn't cold. She turned back around and Jordan was leaning against the wall drinking a beer. She was wearing faded blue jeans, a tight black t-shirt, and black leather shoes. A young blond-haired girl was standing very close to her. Callie couldn't help being excited and terribly jealous at the same time. Jordan hadn't noticed the doctor sitting across from her at the bar. Slowly Callie made her way through the crowd and backed up to the wall next to Jordan.

"I see you're not-"

"A chicken? Of course I'm not. I just wanted to finish my paperwork. I'm sorry I have an important job that I take seriously," Jordan said sarcastically.

"Buy me a drink since you seem to have the most important job in here. You must be made of gold as well." The two of them were so busy arguing, neither one noticed that the woman that was standing there talking with Jordan had walked away.

"You know something, Doctor?"

"What, Lieutenant? What can you possibly tell me? Is this another lecture?"

"No, are you always a smart ass? I was going to say how did you hear of this place? I've never seen a bar that has an area for everyone."

"I met the owner in the hotel bar. By the way, how did you know to find me in this room?" Callie asked.

"I wasn't looking for you. I actually thought you wouldn't be in here." She wasn't sure if Callie was a lesbian, or bi, or just playing with her head so she could get the information she wanted on the case. She figured that room would be last room Callie would be in,

"I see, so you were going to take little Miss High School, barely legal, back to your room," Callie sneered.

"And you were going to leave with Mister Ed, to be

her bitch," Jordan laughed.

"Piss off!" Callie stomped her way back over to the bar to get another beer. Just as she went to pay Jordan appeared, standing right up against her as she reached across Callie's shoulder and handed a five dollar bill to the bartender.

"This one's on me," she said. She didn't mean to upset Callie, just playfully get back at her.

The two of them sat there in silence drinking their beers. Callie was enraged. She believed she deserved a very minimal amount of it. She was raging more at the fact that Jordan had called her bluff. Callie couldn't handle sitting there silently. She walked out on to the dance floor, not a second later a woman similar to the one that she'd been talking to before came over and started dancing with her. Jordan sat at the bar with her back to them not wanting to watch the dark haired doctor in another woman's arms. After her third beer she stood up and paid the tab, never turning around as she left the bar. Callie returned to the hotel soon after Jordan to find that she had gone to bed.

~

Their plane left on schedule. Jordan once again was sitting by the window and Callie closely by her side. She liked the fact that they had to sit so close together. Callie liked it too, although she wasn't about to let on that she felt that way. Callie fell asleep in the middle of the flight, facing the aisle instead of Jordan.

Jordan was never able to sleep on airplanes. She didn't like them very much and decided she wanted to be alert at all times. She asked the flight attendant to get a blanket for Callie. She knew she would get cold since she had taken her jacket off when they boarded. Throughout the long trip back across the country she sat there pondering different thoughts of the last three days she'd spent with this woman. *What a wild character, sleek, harsh, yet inevitably sensitive.*

Jordan watched her sleep; her long dark hair had fallen into her face. Her chest rose with every breath of air, and back down as she exhaled. She was losing herself to this woman. She knew she had to break ties with her soon. Jordan could never let the doctor know the ghosts of her past. No one knew them personally, except herself.

~

"While you were away playing with phonies I took the liberty to question a few of the leads that were called in," Lance said. I also ran our MO through NCIC with the FBI, but nothing came up. I hope you came back with something we can use."

Jordan wasn't happy. She didn't much care for Lance or his attitude. Being a babysitter was neither in her resume nor her job description. *Something we can use, you little shit, you're about as close to this case as I am to being straight! You don't think I already looked in NCIC? How stupid do you think I am? Damn you Osborne, next time you can baby sit.*

She had come back with intuition and no solid answers. She sat at her small metal desk with Callie's face poised on the back of her mind. She had a feeling that somehow, somewhere, sometime very soon, this guy was going to strike again.

~

Jordan settled back into her natural form of everyday secluded, single, lonely workaholic life, after being back for a week. On Friday night she went up to the Beer Cellar to have a beer after leaving the long work week behind. As soon as she stepped inside, her cell phone rang. Instinct told her it was Captain Osborne before she even looked down at the caller ID.

"I think we have victim number four, Jordan. Meet us at Pier 2," he said.

She ran back down to the trolley since she hadn't driven the patrol car and she had no time to go back to get it. She rode all the way to the end of California Street and walked up through Justin Herman Plaza.

Callie was there speaking with Lance who had also been called. Jordan walked right past both of them and down onto the pier where the body was lying. Sure enough it was a blond female wrapped in a white sheet with the slashing cuts, a gunshot wound, and severely beaten skull.

"Who reported this?" Jordan asked.

"One of the ferry boats saw her floating out in the middle. They brought her up here," A patrol officer said.

"Any other witnesses?"

"No Ma'am," he said.

Callie walked up behind Jordan watching her go over every detail. She always changed into a different person at the scene, especially around the bodies.

"Lance, let's make sure this end of the pier and that ferry boat are completely taped off. No one comes in or around twenty feet of here or the boat. I want a patrol detail here all night and no media or civilians of any kind around until we can safely secure the scene in the morning. Dr. Marceau, I'll be meeting the body back at the morgue, don't start your examination until I can be there," Jordan said and walked back up the dock towards the trolley.

Callie wanted to follow her, but she knew it was best to leave her alone. She was in her own world, almost like she was grieving. It was extremely painful to watch her eyes grow solemnly dark as she transformed into this personality that nearly frightened Callie. She wondered if somehow Jordan was able to feel this guy, like it was a personal vendetta between them. She had never seen a detective get so involved in a case, living and feeling everything in the file, from the killer to the victim, except for her father who gave his life to his cases. The memories of him and his work haunted her day in and day out. She was starting to see part of his hypnotized behavior coming out in Jordan's nonconforming personality.

~

"I need to know everything you can tell me about this woman. I'm prepared to stay as long as possible." Jordan spoke sternly.

Callie couldn't help staring into the detectives pain filled eyes. Jordan watched intensively as the doctor performed by the book procedures exposing the woman's murderous secrets one by one.

Four hours later, the data turned up the first link, the bullet was a perfect match to the others. Jordan paced back and forth in the large cold room. She never spoke, only monitored every word out of Callie's soft blush colored lips. Her mind slipped away from the chilling array of events long enough to feel the sensation of kissing that desirable, passionate mouth. *Damn it Jordan you have to concentrate. He won't stop until he gets you. You have to get him first.*

Callie turned towards Jordan who was standing against the wall on the opposite side of the room.

"She's number four, Detective. The incisions were all made by the same instruments as the other three bodies. The fractures to the skull were made with a similar object if not the same. The sheet has the same fiber content and her hair is naturally blond."

Jordan stood silent for a moment lost in thought.

"Thank you. I'll be back later for the complete file," she said before leaving the room.

Jordan headed down the long gray hallway to the elevator door and down to the garage and her unmarked black cruiser. She drove across town and parked at the edge of the curb by the Pier 2 gate. The uniformed patrol was still guarding the yellow tape. She sat there for nearly an hour running through the case file in her head before slowly stepping out onto the asphalt slamming the car door shut.

As she ducked under the first tape crossing she noticed someone standing on the end of the pier on the ferry. She knew it was Callie. She didn't notice her arrival and was caught between wanting to go wrap her arms around her to keep her safe and screaming at her for muddling in her investigation. She needed to tell her to leave and stay away from her case. She couldn't stand the angry feelings flowing through her body anymore. She walked down the pier and stopped right behind the woman.

"You shouldn't be here. Don't make me call McCormick," Jordan said.

Callie turned around almost into Jordan's arms. "I need to be here as much as you do. This isn't about you, Jordan. I want to catch this guy too. I can help you and you know it." Jordan stood close enough to feel the heat radiating off of Callie's body.

"Dr. Marceau, if I thought you could help me, or even be a part of this investigation I would let you know. Now it appears to me that I have neither asked for your help nor do I intend to. If you would please leave this crime scene, not only would it be in your best interest, but it would be greatly appreciated. It's not safe here." Jordan said backing away. She followed Callie's lead to the front of the pier.

Callie desperately wanted to press her to talk. She knew there was something eating away at the detective, something deeper than this case could ever be.

~

A week went by, Jordan went to the gym and office everyday as usual and made it a point to avoid running into the woman that was driving her crazy. It felt a little odd not running into Callie somewhere or needing to talk to her about something pertaining to the case. Jordan figured it was one small flicker of luck that life would let her have a peaceful week. On Friday night she packed her dreadful paperwork and files into her leather, zippered briefcase and proceeded down the hall to the elevator. She swore she could sense Callie's presence, but she was nowhere around.

She walked into the luxury hotel suite she called home throwing her suit jacket over the arm of the chair in the living room. In her bedroom she unhooked the holster at her side and pulled the straps forward over her shoulders placing the gun in the wall safe still snapped in its case. She quickly changed into jeans and a long sleeve, Henley style, dark blue shirt. She wore a black tank top under the blue shirt that was made for concealing a weapon. It had a small holster pocket under the right arm that fit her small 9MM back-up weapon perfectly. She put her ID badge into her back pocket and walked out the door.

She rode the trolley over to Polk Street and walked a block to Kim's Penthouse Showroom. She was just in time for the start of the drag queen entertainment show of the night. She hopped up on a bar stool and ordered a beer. She still couldn't remove Callie's face from the back of her mind. She stopped watching the show when she began focusing on the pictures playing in her head. She remembered the last time she touched another woman. It was so long ago, another time, another city, another Jordan. Her body and soul longed for that lustful exciting feeling of pleasure. Her mind pushed it away. *You're not going to let her win. You have to be stronger. She will get hurt. You can't let him hurt her.*

The horrible reflections of her past disintegrated the beautiful thoughts of Callie. She felt incredibly cold, like a ghost, as the dark images from her past took her back into a different time and place. She dropped her beer as her body started to shiver. The bartender quickly reached across and grabbed her ice cold hands. He knew she wasn't drunk; she hadn't even finished the first beer. Realizing where she was, she rapidly stood up apologizing for her actions and raced out of the bar to the fresh air, barely making it around the corner struggling to catch her breath. All she could see was his face spinning around a helpless body lying on the ground. The face of the body had changed from the one in her memory to Callie's. She dropped to her knees just in time as the vomit flew from her mouth onto the grass.

Rubbing her mouth, the spell was over. Her mind was blank. There was nothing there, no sound, no picture. It vanished as quickly as it appeared. Luckily, it was late and no one was out on the street. She hadn't had an episode that terrifying in over a year. She didn't want to recall the details, pushing that night as far back as she could into her mind instead.

CHAPTER FOUR

"Jordan, I can't just let you take a leave of absence in the middle of an investigation. Are you crazy? I need you here on top of this guy. You can take a vacation when you catch him," Captain Osborne said.

"With all due respect, Captain, I can't tell you where or why. I just have to go. If I don't go I may not be able to solve this case, it's for my own good. Please understand I'm not doing this to jeopardize myself, this case, or your career. You have to trust me."

"Jordan..." he hissed.

"Captain, at least let me take a couple of days off. I'll be back next Monday. If he strikes again or something serious comes up I will be available."

He knew he wasn't going to win this argument. He also knew the woman standing in front of him was chasing ghosts much bigger than he could ever imagine. "Look Jordan, you're going to be sick for the rest of the week as far as I'm concerned. You will return healthy and forget this ever happened. Got that?"

She left his office surprised that things had gone slightly easier than she predicted. She couldn't leave town like she planned, but a couple of days away from work might help her clear the demons from her mind.

Jordan spent the next two days doing almost nothing. She went to the gym and swam a few laps, other than that she lounged around her suite eating frozen pizza and watching movies and sports on the TV. She avoided the news at all costs. The only time her phone rang was when Callie called. She reluctantly sent the calls to her voicemail.

~

Callie asked Lance where Jordan had been when she saw him on Friday. She hadn't seen her nor spoken to Jordan in over a week.

"She was out yesterday and today. Captain Osborne said she was sick. She's supposed to be back Monday though."

Callie knew better than that. She also knew Jordan was too close to the case. Jordan was gone. She was running from something, not answering her phone for days, not working frantically around the clock. It wasn't rational. Callie wished she knew how to find her, but the detective had gone completely off the map.

Callie called and left the reclusive detective another voicemail. "Jordan, it's Callie, please return my call. I'm worried about you. Lance says you're sick. I've only known you for a few months and you're as healthy as a horse. Anyway, I want to help you with this. Together we can get this asshole. Please, Jordan, give me a chance. I'm a phone call away. Always." *Callie, you've definitely lost your mind. Who's to say she even feels the same way about you? I mean you know she's a lesbian or at least you're pretty sure she is and up until a few weeks ago you thought you were straight, go figure.*

Callie hung up the phone somehow hoping that Jordan would just listen. The despair in her voice was obvious; she was worried about Jordan's mental health as well as her safety. She knew Jordan felt the unavoidable passion slowly drawing them together. Since Jordan wouldn't talk to her, she had no choice but to utilize her other information sources to find out about the mysterious woman. She dialed another number.

"Eric, it's Callie. I need some information," she said.

"Callie? It's been a long time, are you in trouble?" a stern male voice asked.

"No, I think a friend may be though. Her name is Jordan Denali and she's a Detective for SFPD. I need anything and everything you can get on her as soon as possible."

"It'll take some time, internal documents are hard to dredge up."

"Thanks."

"I wish you would leave him in the past, Callie. The only time I hear from my baby sister is when you're sticking your nose where it doesn't belong."

"I promise this time it has nothing to do with dad," Callie said hanging up the phone. *I'll help her whether she wants me to or not. I can't stop myself. She has a powerful possession over me and she doesn't even know it.*

~

Jordan was tired of feeling the torture of being away from work. Taking a few days for herself did make things slightly easier in her mind. Now, if it would only stay that way. She knew he would be back, his ghost overpowered her. It was her job to catch this killer and put her ghosts to rest and she was prepared to take whatever came her way, without the help of Callie or Lance.

55

Jordan finally ventured out to the coffee shop on Sunday and was sitting at a small round table in the corner enjoying an iced coffee when her cell phone rang. It was an unusual number and she didn't feel like talking to anyone until Monday, so she didn't answer. The phone beeped once to show a voicemail message had been left, she ignored it picking up the paper on the table. She was amazed at the write up on the Bay City Killer in the headlines. Apparently, the reporters thought the killer was a female, as well as homeless, and the detective on the case was a male. Also, the only weapon was a shotgun.

"What is this shit?" She couldn't help laughing out loud at the ridiculous nonsense in the paper. "I guess this is what happens when your team does a great job of stopping media coverage." She felt her head swell a bit thinking of the great job she had done, unfortunately she would have to contact the newspaper and get things straightened out. *I'll deal with this issue tomorrow. Right now I'm going to enjoy the fact that everyone in town is reading this, including Captain Osborne. If I could only see the look on his face.*

Later on that night she checked the saved message. The voice on the other end was Callie's. She was apparently calling from her house, once again asking to be involved in the case and was checking to see if Jordan was still alive. Jordan wanted to call her back just to hear her talk. *We've been through this, you know you can't control the emotions, but you can damn sure control your actions. Leave her alone.*

~

The alarm went off at five a.m. causing Jordan to jump clear out of her bed. She was wide awake ready to knock someone out. "Goddamn alarm clock," She said tossing it across the room against the wall. She put on her gym clothes and headed out the door.

A few hours later she was showered and dressed in one of her dark gray pant suits. She had on a button down black shirt under the jacket that was slightly open just enough to show her upper chest, but not too revealing and certainly not showing cleavage. She walked into the elevator, pushing the number for her floor.

Jordan was feeling slightly nervous not knowing everything that had gone on in her week long absence. The doors opened and she walked passed a few people telling her they were glad she was back and sorry to hear she had gotten sick. The Captain was in his office when she entered his doorway. He asked her to kindly shut the door behind her and have a seat. The hair on the back of her neck stood up. *Here we go.*

"I want you to know I'm glad you're back. I need you to be here, healthy and free of whatever it is that's been bothering you. We can't stop this asshole without you, Jordan. I do believe you know this. I'm only telling you because you need to hear it from someone other than yourself. I've known you for just over three years. I've seen you solve some of the toughest cases and catch some of the worst criminals, but not once have I ever seen you this involved. Be careful, Jordan. Sometimes the best need help too."

"Yes, Sir. I'm glad to be back. I'm here to do a job. This is what I'm paid for. I have a lot of catching up to do today. I..."

"I think you should go down to the newspaper and

get them straight. You wouldn't believe what they've been putting out for their readers," he said shaking his head.

"I saw it. I know I have to fix it, but I still think it was funny. Where the hell do they get this stuff?"

"I don't know just take care of it. Have Lance call them."

She nodded and walked out of the room towards her own office when Lance stepped out of his cubical in front of her.

"Yes, can I help you?" she said.

"Well, you can start by returning a call or two. Everyone was worried about you, especially Dr. Marceau. She asked everyday if I had heard from you. I guess you weren't returning her calls either. How are we...?"

"Look, what I do on my own time is my business. I was sick and didn't feel like talking to anyone. I'm back and the god damn walls are still standing. The bodies are still in the morgue, the killer is still on the loose, and nothing has changed. I don't need a lecture from a rookie! Now, if you would please excuse me, I have work to do."

"I don't care what you do. I'm getting paid just as you are to work on this case. I do think you should go see Dr. Marceau or at least call her. She may have some new information. She wouldn't share it with me if she did anyway," he said.

"You want to help me with something on this case? Call the newspaper and give them a semi-straighter story than the one they have printed today. The Captain's not too happy about the headlines," Jordan said walking into her office.

She sat at her desk, kicking her feet up onto the edge of the metal corner. It felt good to be back. She needed to regain control before she faced the enemy. Callie would know something was up, she wasn't stupid. How would she go about talking to her without letting on that she was right the whole time? Callie was a smart woman, very, very smart. She put her feet down and opened up all of the files laying them out on her desk. Everything matched so closely. All of the women were basically identical. Their looks, wounds, expressions, lives, all so close together. Maybe Callie did have something helpful. Jordan knew she needed something more. This guy was becoming impossible to catch. Her intuition kept telling her he would return.

Jordan knew it was part of her job to go to the M.E.'s office on a regular basis to check for information. She just didn't want it to be part of her job to run into the dark-haired doctor every day. *Okay here we go, fly like a butterfly, sting like a bee, fight like hell. She can smell fear, Jordan!*

~

Chloe was standing in front of the elevator when the doors opened. "Well, hello there, Detective. How are you?"

"I'm great and you?" Jordan said.

"I'm fantastic, trust me," she said with a wink as she stepped into the elevator.

Jordan was a little embarrassed at the straight-aimed, clearly sexual gesture Chloe had just shot towards her. She turned back around shaking it off as she walked further down the hall. She heard the voice she had been longing to hear. Callie came out of the exam room talking into a small recorder. She stopped dead in her tracks.

Jordan's blue eyes lit up as she stared directly at Callie. She couldn't speak, her body surrendered, overcome by desire. *So much for fighting like hell, Jordan, you sorry ass.*

Callie wanted to throw her arms around the detective's neck and press their lips together. She tamped down the attractive feelings long enough to find her voice.

"The infamous Lieutenant returns. It's about time you caught up to this case. I thought you were abducted by aliens. Woody...Lance, yes, that's his name, Lance told me aliens picked you up out on the pier and they would bring you back today. I guess he was right."

"I'm sorry I..."

"No, don't be sorry. It's not my place to hear it, nor do I want to. We need to get this fourth file taken care of. You were abducted before I could finish my notes on it."

As they walked into Callie's office she handed Jordan a manila envelope from her filing cabinet. Jordan set it down on the desk.

"Here is your file, Detective. I hope everything is to your liking. This guy is good. I think maybe he's had help from someone or maybe directions and training. It feels like an M.O. that I've seen before, but as far as I can tell he's not copying anyone else's work. I've looked back into autopsy files for California on the computer as far back as ten years ago and nothing comes up."

Jordan was glad she had only looked at the records for this state. She hoped Callie wouldn't go as far as digging through her past cases. Nothing in the files could help her anyway. Jordan wanted to straighten out the confusion separating her and Callie. She would never forget the moment that passed between them in Florida. It was still lingering in her dreams at night.

"I believe this is all you were looking for. Now, if you would excuse me, I have some other things to take care of. I am glad to see the aliens returned you in one piece. Maybe next time they'll let you have one phone call back to Earth," Callie said sarcastically as she opened the office door and walked out.

Jordan felt terrible. The pain was clear in Callie's eyes. She was hurt. Jordan had caused this sad rift between them. It would be too dangerous for Callie to know the truth. That would probably hurt her even worse. Jordan would need to continue pushing the secrets of her past down deep so they couldn't hurt anyone.

~

Jordan drove the unmarked car back to Pier 2 hoping to comb over something she missed in the first search. She walked aimlessly around the pier. Frustrated when she didn't find anything, she left there and went back to the Bay Bridge. The fourth woman was more than likely dropped over the side like the first two. Why had he chosen the Golden Gate for the third woman? There was something special about her. Maybe he knew her?

For hours Jordan wandered around the Bridge, not realizing she had walked down one side and back up the other. Her mind was lost in images of the dark-haired woman that seemed to invade her every thought and every dream. Jordan wanted to hold her, just once, long enough to make the feeling of holding her and the images in her head real. She had spent a week hoping to clear Callie from her head. Nothing was helping, not even the trip out of town. It was her job to keep people safe, how would she continue to keep the doctor safe if she didn't stop getting so involved? Jordan knew if Callie found out the truth about this case as well as her past she would never let her forget about it. All she wanted to do was forget. She seemed to remember more than she forgot most of the time.

~

Callie was standing in the elevator as Jordan entered. Neither woman spoke to the other on their way to the ground floor. Jordan wanted to talk to her, but she didn't know what to say or how to say it.

Callie was still upset. The elusive detective seemed to hurt her more and more. She began to wonder if it was worth it. Jordan was sexy as hell with her beautiful, arousing blue eyes and cocky grin. Callie looked up at Jordan. The detective had this horribly sad look in her eyes behind the tough girl facade that Callie could see right through. Callie wanted to know why she felt that way. What made her so secretive? She reminded Callie so much of her own father before he died.

The elevator door opened and they both shot out of the there like it was on fire, running from the pain of being close to the other. The tension between them was so startling they were overtaken by claustrophobia inside their heads, both tearing and scratching at the walls in their minds to get out.

Jordan went left. Callie went right, before turning around realizing she needed to take the trolley since she didn't drive to work that morning. She caught up to Jordan at the waiting line. Jordan noticed Callie standing silently behind her at the curb.

Jordan jumped off and walked a block over to the tower she was living in on top of Nob Hill. Callie stayed aboard to catch the California connection, which ran a few blocks closer to the location of the Victorian townhouse she rented.

~

Jordan walked into her suite, tossing her briefcase on the rectangle shaped table and her suit jacket across the dining room chair. The Venetian blinds were still turned halfway open to the view of the city lights with the bay flowing behind them. She unstrapped the gun holster from around her shoulders and set it down with her badge in their usual place on the nightstand next to her bed. Her clothes flew off one piece at a time while she rushed around the bathroom preparing to take a shower.

An hour later, Jordan walked out of the lobby heading back towards the trolley stop. As soon as she stepped onto the cable car her phone began to vibrate in her pocket. She didn't feel much like talking especially to Lance so she hit the voicemail button figuring he was probably whining again. The trolley came to a stop and she jumped off.

The Buena Vista Cafe was lit up on the corner. Looking forward to having a beer and putting an end to her long week, she walked across the street and into the bar. It was just beginning to fill up. The woman behind the counter asked what she was drinking as Jordan sat down on the stool in front of her.

"Beer, please." *I'd kill for a glass of Scotch right about now, but I'm not feeling that miserable, yet.*

After finishing her first beer and listening to the band

play a few songs she'd never heard, she noticed Callie sitting at a table alone across from her. She asked for two more beers and paid the tab before walking over to the small round table. *I'm not looking for a best friend, a lover, or even a close friend. I'm merely making nice with a woman I have to deal with at work.* She tried to give herself some sort of excuse for walking over to Callie, who hadn't even noticed her at the bar anyway.

She stopped at the table, poised with two beer bottles in her hand in front of Callie.

"May I sit?"

The dark-haired woman looked up with shimmering green eyes and fought off a smile as she kicked the chair out with her foot.

"Okay, I guess that's a yes," Jordan said.

Callie was sitting there almost as comfortable as she had been in the lesbian bar wearing jeans and a tight black v-neck shirt under a black leather jacket. Callie couldn't help noticing the long sleeve, button down shirt. The collar was loosely open and unbuttoned down to the spot just above the indention between her breasts. A gold chain hung just below her collar bone.

"So, Detective, what brings you to my table? Are we trying to redeem ourselves?" Callie asked. "Or are you following me?"

"Well, I would like to share a beer with you," she said handing the second beer to Callie.

"If this is your sad attempt to let me know that you have a job to do and I need to keep to myself I'm going to tell you to shove it up your ass, okay?"

"Callie, calm down, I'm not here to..."

"Oh yes you are. It's pretty obvious you don't care who you hurt as long as you solve your case. Detective

Denali, I noticed this side of you when we met. I hoped I would never be introduced to it."

"Why exactly are you so bitter towards me?"

"Well, let's see, you have been ignoring me for how long now? Since we met, yes that's right. I'm supposed to be working with you. Do you remember? Also, you think the goddamn world revolves around Jordan Denali, well news goddamn flash, it doesn't! You have a serious problem and you need help," Callie growled.

She had let herself get so entangled in her feelings for Jordan that it was starting to hurt terribly to feel the rejection from the detective day in and day out. She couldn't stop the words from flying out of her mouth. She wanted Jordan to feel the hurt and the pain she was feeling deep inside as she was lusting for this woman that wouldn't have her.

"I don't have a problem and I don't need help. Can you please just be civil for once? I know I upset you. I'm sorry for that. I take my job seriously, Callie, and I work alone. I have my reasons and I just wish you would understand. I want a civil relationship with you. I have to deal with seeing you at work and I don't want you to be so angry at me all of the time because I don't speak to you about my personal life. I'm sorry. It's my personality. I can't help it." Jordan said.

She wanted to kiss Callie terribly. Arguing with her was driving the heart rate up causing the wetness to flow between her legs. Jordan stood up finishing her last beer and setting it back onto the table.

"Callie, I hope you understand I'm protecting you. This is my job. Like it or not, I have taken a sworn oath to uphold the law, to serve and protect, and I'm bound and determined to keep it. It doesn't concern you. I'm sorry if I made you feel like it did. My cases are my life, please stay out of them. Have a good night." Jordan turned and walked out of the bar.

Callie sat there with a horrible look on her face. She had just seen Jordan's eyes change drastically from warm and bright to a dark, cold and lonely stare. She jumped up and headed for the door looking outside for Jordan in both directions. She spotted her walking towards the trolley and ran after her, just making it. As the cable car started to move she jumped on the outside rail next to Jordan.

"Look, I want to talk to you. Will you stop and get some coffee with me? Maybe take a walk?" She was hoping Jordan would agree, things needed to be resolved between them before they returned to work Monday morning.

"Fine," Jordan said without making eye contact.

They hopped off at the next stop grabbing a hot cup of coffee to help warm the night air and began walking south down Larkin Street, still barely speaking.

"I want you to know I've had a bad few days and I didn't mean to take it out on you, Jordan. It's just...I want in on this case and every time I get close you cause a conflict. I didn't mean to lay into you back there. I had no right. I'm sorry," Callie said.

"I understand you want to work on this case as well. If you would just listen to me. This is a serial killer investigation and if you haven't noticed I'm in charge. I'm sorry if that offends you, but I work by the book." *Alone.*

"Okay, let's try to get past this then. I'm still going to be there right beside you at the next place we end up. Like it or not. Do what you have to do, Lieutenant. I have my own reasons for wanting to help with this investigation."

Callie noticed how different Jordan looked away from work. Like another person. She couldn't resist the way Jordan made her feel. She'd never been so passionately drawn to anyone, especially not a woman.

Jordan was always the dominant one. She found it very arousing when Callie stepped up to be just as bold and aggressive. It was why she walked away in the first place. She needed to be in control and Callie was learning how to override that control.

"This is my block. Would you like to walk me home since you seem to be such a protector and everything, and these streets are so unsafe?" Callie smiled as she poked fun at Jordan.

Jordan laughing slightly and walked her right up to the door.

~

Callie put the key in lock, opened the door and moved into the foyer. Jordan followed her lead inside. Callie reached behind Jordan shutting the door and pushing Jordan up against it with her body pressed tightly to Jordan's. Jordan couldn't think fast enough to stop her. The feminine folds between her legs were swollen, painfully aching to be touched. Callie pressed her mouth against Jordan's as she ran her hands through her short hair. Jordan wrapped her arms around Callie's waist, pulling her tightly and pressing her thigh between Callie's legs. Their tongues dueled as their bodies pulsated from head to toe. They were molded together from head to toe rubbing against each other like teenagers.

Jordan pushed Callie away just enough to break the

contact between their bodies, fighting to catch her breath.

"Callie...I...can't. I can't do this I'm sorry."

Jordan didn't want to stop. Her body was drawing her back to Callie. She couldn't calm the sensation between her legs. She wanted to be with this woman. She longed for her. She knew she had to break the contact before it was too late.

Callie was surprised at the reaction from Jordan. "You know you don't want to stop. Don't do this, Jordan!" Callie's body was screaming for pleasure before her mind could come into focus.

"I...can't Callie. I'm sorry, goodnight." Jordan quickly turned and walked out the door. Callie turned the lock as she watched through the peep hole. She couldn't get the feeling out of her head. Jordan's lips felt so soft and warm. They fit perfectly to hers. *Well, it wasn't my first kiss with a woman, but it was definitely the best! Why is she so god damn stubborn? I felt it, she feels the same way. Why are you fighting so hard Jordan? Who is it? What is it? Watching you like this is driving me insane, you're like goddamn Jekyll and Hyde.*

~

Jordan wasn't able to stop the pictures replaying in her head. Callie's gentle delicate body in her arms. Her lips, wet with desire. *Oh god Jordan, you let her get to you. Damn you, Jordan. Damn you!* Jordan hadn't felt another body against hers in so long. She could hardly walk to the trolley station as the throbbing between her thighs subsided very slowly. She had almost forgotten what it felt like to hold another woman in her arms. Somehow, it still felt so wrong. The ghosts of her past weren't going to leave her alone.

Thank god it was Friday. She would have the weekend to think of something to say to Callie on Monday. Hopefully not upsetting her or making a fool of herself. She could never tell her the truth. Jordan believed her past would hurt Callie, possibly turn her away forever.

CHAPTER FIVE

Jordan was sitting in her office reviewing the assortment of files in the Bay City Killer case when the Captain came rushing through her door. The look on his face revealed to her something she had almost been waiting for. She didn't hesitate, nor did she show any remorse.

"Where is she?"

"Over at Baker Beach. She washed ashore a few minutes ago. Patrol said she looks like one of ours," he said.

"I'm on it," Jordan said pushing past him and walking briskly towards the elevator. She ran over to her cruiser and took off with the siren wailing and the small dash light flashing.

Jordan knew she would eventually have to see Callie, she just wasn't sure if she was ready. All of her focus needed to be on this killer, he had to be stopped. She'd have to put a stop to her feelings for Callie. *I can't let him hurt you. I have to protect you from him. No matter how bad I want to be with you, I can't, I don't want to lose you.*

~

Jordan saw a detail of patrol officers gathered around a spot down in the sand on the beach. Callie was there with them, as well as Lance, who ironically rode with her.

Jordan trudged through the sand and made her way down to the young woman lying in the bloody sheet next to the water. The victim looked identical to the other four. She felt this terrible pain take over her stomach. She immediately turned and walked back about thirty feet and began vomiting uncontrollably.

Callie ran quickly to her side.

"Jordan, are you ok?" Callie's hands were on Jordan's shoulders giving her leverage to lean back on. Jordan's body was quivering slightly.

"Should I call the paramedics down here, Doctor?" Lance came rushing over to check on his partner.

"No, Lance, she'll be fine. Everyone back up and give her some room please. Thanks," Callie said. "Jordan, can you talk to me? Please? What happened to you? I've never seen you react like this. Are you feeling ok?"

Jordan put her hand on top of Callie's, which was still resting on her shoulder. She felt partly embarrassed and partly scared to death. He was definitely getting closer to her. Whoever this was, his work was getting better and better. It felt comforting having Callie right there holding on to her.

"I'm fine, Doctor, thanks. Can you leave me alone for a minute...please? I'll be ok, I just need some air." Jordan stood up straight and walked back up to her car. She leaned against it for a few minutes trying to regain what little control she had.

Callie walked back over to the body where everyone was standing. "I guess she must've eaten at that nasty Mexican place by the station. She'll be ok. Watch where you step over there," Callie said trying to be somewhat humorous, knowing it was damn good and well, not something she ate. Jordan's secrets were getting darker as she became closer to her. Why? She couldn't understand the mystery behind this person she was falling so deeply for.

Jordan walked back down the hill to the body and the small group of people hovering over her. "Sorry guys, lunch got a little carried away. We need to get this going. It's very critical since she probably wasn't in the water all that long. Callie, I need this body back to the morgue and the autopsy needs to be as soon as possible. Also, Lance make sure the patrol detail stays here. I want this beach combed for evidence. I also want boats. As many damn boats as you can get searching the water. Another thing, we need the Golden Gate Bridge swept for evidence as well. He definitely dropped her from there probably sometime last night. I'll be on my cell if anyone needs me." Turning Jordan walked back up the hill towards the car.

From her squat near the body Callie looked over her shoulder. "Lance, you're going to need a ride back. I have to go prepare for the body coming in."

"Hey, Jordan," Lance said running up the sandy hill with Callie walking behind him. "I'm going to need the car. I don't want the patrol guys to have to stop searching to run me places."

"Oh yeah, I'm sorry I forgot. Here take my keys. Callie, would you mind giving me a ride back to the station?"

"No, I don't mind at all. I'm headed there now. It'll cost you five bucks though." She smiled at Jordan. Of course she wouldn't mind. It would give her a few minutes alone with her.

As soon as the car began moving, Callie opened her mouth to speak and Jordan was right there to stop her. She wanted to hold her again, feel her warm body. Callie felt like pulling over and forcing Jordan to talk but she knew the detective would clam back up into her shell. Her eyes grew very dark out on the beach and they remained that way the entire drive back.

"I would appreciate it if you wouldn't say anything, Callie. I have enough on my mind to deal with. I'm fine. I had a bad lunch, seeing the blood made it come up."

"Have you ever talked to someone about all of the stress your under? A therapist maybe?"

"Trust me. I'm fine. Please drop it. This doesn't concern you."

~

Jordan sat back in the chair behind her desk, trying to get the images of that body out of her head. Somehow, this case was connected to her past. She knew she had to figure out the connection in order to catch the sick bastard. She read carefully over every note in the file comparing likes and differences in every victim and crime scene. *He's good, but I've got to be better at his game to beat him.*

Lance called to let her know the Bridge had been cleared, they found nothing useful there. The crime scene was almost finished and the boats in the water came up dry. *Damn it, you have to give me something.*

When the body arrived Jordan went up to oversee the autopsy. Callie was in her office reading all of her notes from each examination. Everything was a match. She couldn't understand the guy's motive. It had something to do with beautiful, petite, and young, blond-haired women. Did they piss him off; remind him of something he didn't like? She wasn't sure how Jordan's past was involved, but she knew somehow it was.

Jordan knocked on the closed frosted glass door.

"Come in," Callie said. She was sitting at her desk finishing a report.

"I assume everything is ready to go. I'm looking for anything and everything we can get," Jordan said. "There has to be something we can use to catch this bastard."

"I was waiting for you. We're all set up."

Jordan was in a different tone of voice when she spoke. Every victim seemed to drag her lower. Callie had seen her reactions to three separate bodies. Jordan's rage worsened with every new homicide. The pain in her blue eyes was unbearable for Callie to watch.

"As far as I could tell at the scene, she'd been in the water less than twenty-four hours. We should be able to get a little more detail."

Callie began the excruciating exam of the body. Jordan stood back from the table watching every move the doctor made. The pain grew deeper in Jordan as Callie opened the eye lids of the woman. The eyes behind them were baby blue, almost gray. Jordan turned away rapidly as she noticed the color. Callie wrote her notes and quickly closed the lids back down. Jordan excused herself for a few minutes and stepped out into the hall. She sat down on the small iron bench outside the doorway. *Why? Why are you doing this to me? Please let her go. It's over.* She couldn't stop a small tear from escaping her left eye. She wiped it away before anyone noticed. About fifteen minutes later, Jordan walked back into the exam room.

"Are you ok, Detective? You still seem a little shook up from this morning," Callie said. She couldn't help but wonder if it was because of the passionate kiss they'd shared a few nights before.

Jordan shrugged it off. "I'm fine. Just a little tired that's all."

"You don't have to stay here. I can do this without you. The results will be back from a few of the tests in a few hours. I'll call you when I know something. You should go home and get some sleep." Callie said. She tried to console her the best way she could, without pushing the subject. Jordan was obviously dealing with something larger than she wanted to admit. Callie wasn't a therapist, but she was starting to wonder if Jordan was suffering from PTSD.

"No. I'm fine, please continue. I have to be here, whether I want to or not, it's my job to catch this guy. I have to stop him." Jordan's voice was deadly serious as she spoke.

Callie felt a small shudder throughout her body, slightly making her nervous with fear. Jordan's actions changed drastically with every new victim. These changes were one of the most frightening things Callie had ever seen in a person.

The room remained in a cold silence for the next hour as Callie continued the examination. Neither woman made eye contact. Callie stared at the corpse on the table in front of her as she worked carefully. She noticed the detective pacing the room off and on out the corner of her eye.

Jordan left the floor when Callie was finished, returning to her own office to wait for the results that she already knew.

~

Jordan had fallen asleep in her desk chair with her feet propped up on the edge of the desk. Her cell phone rang in her pocket waking her.

"Hello?" Jordan said still half asleep and trying to catch her bearings.

"Jordan, it's Callie. Are you ok?" She was worried, Jordan sounded out of it.

"Oh yeah, I'm fine. I fell asleep at my desk. Damn it. I can't believe I did that. Is there any news, are the tests back?"

"I told you to go home and sleep. You're killing yourself."

"Callie, back off, please, I don't need this from you. I'm on my way up there." She hung up the phone.

Knowing Callie was concerned, made her feel slightly better.

Callie involved herself, therefore she was living with the pain of watching Jordan break down one fraction at a time.

The two women met in the exam room. Jordan couldn't help looking just once into those island green eyes that had been calling for her attention all afternoon.

"Ok, so what do we have?" Jordan said.

"Well, as we thought, she's a match. He's definitely using the same tools, the gun, the blunt object, which we can pretty much say is very similar to a metal bat, and the two scalpels. She was raped post-mortem and the sheet material is the same. He must have a box of condoms he's using as well. The fluids are all the same. There's no semen at all, only a very common form of spermicidal fluid and some of her blood. I think he may be having sex with the bodies as soon as they're dead while they're still warm. He's good at hiding things, but he slipped. We have one very small carpet fiber. It was in her hair, probably from the rape that may have taken place on the floor of his home. It's a popular style carpet, found in most of the Victorian homes throughout San Francisco."

"Ok, at least it's a start." Jordan sighed. "Do we know where these sheets are coming from yet?"

"No, it's a popular material used in most white sheets that are decently priced. We're not talking top of the line, five hundred thread count sheets here, Detective."

"Yes, I know. There has to be something more, something we are all missing," Jordan said.

"Don't beat yourself up over this. We'll get him. I know we will."

"Doctor, I understand what you're trying to do, but..."

"Please, stop calling me Doctor. We've known each other long enough and I damn sure think we are close enough to be on a first name level here," Callie growled with a small twitching in her foot. She hated being called doctor. It was so formal, nothing like her personality at all.

"I need to get back to my paperwork. I'll contact you tomorrow morning for the notes on the file." Jordan didn't acknowledge anything that Callie had just said to her as she stepped out of the room. She had to make herself act by the book, otherwise her feelings would take over and she couldn't bear to let Callie get hurt.

~

Jordan went straight home from the M.E.'s office

stopping to grab her briefcase from her desk on the way out. She couldn't stop the terror in her mind and the desire her body was drowning in at the same time.

She took a long, hot shower, before pouring herself a small neat glass of scotch. The carafe set was sitting on the bar waiting for a night when she needed to take the pain away. She sipped it slowly as she sat down on the couch, her tanned skin nude under a short, charcoal gray, silk robe. She turned the TV on. There was nothing but the news speaking of the newly found body on every channel. She turned it off and moved back against the cushion curling her feet up.

She woke up at two a.m. when she rolled over falling off of the couch and onto the carpeted floor. "Ouch! Damn coffee table," she growled rubbing her sore back where she crashed into the table.

She sat back up on the couch noticing the carafe of scotch over at the bar and the empty glass in front of her. She contemplated pouring another glass, but took her robe off and slowly made her way to bed instead.

At five a.m. the alarm went off. She rolled over to see that it was morning and she hadn't drunk herself into oblivion. She got up and showered quickly before heading down to the gym.

~

Jordan walked out of the elevator wearing a dark blue pants suit with a baby blue colored silk blouse underneath the jacket. It had been twenty-four hours since they found Jenna Rainhan's body floating in the ocean. Jordan knew she wasn't over the exhaustion of the day before. Seeing Callie would more than likely make it worse. *You have to do this, it's your job. No matter how bad you want her, you have to hide it, Jordan.* Her back was against the wall, the feelings running through her body and mind. She ignored the feelings and headed up to her office to pick up some papers she'd left on her desk.

"Good morning, Jordan, I see you're still with us today. I heard you weren't feeling well yesterday. Is everything ok?" The captain snuck out of his office long enough to check on his prize performer.

"Yes, I was a little under my lunch. I'm fine now," she said.

Jordan walked by Lance's cubical. He looked up and smiled quickly as she passed. *Hmm, wonder what's up his sleeve. Whatever it is, it can't be good.* She thought making her way into the elevator before the doors shut. She was whisked up two floors and the doors swung open. She stepped out to see Callie standing a few feet away wearing blue scrubs. She always had them on during the autopsies; Jordan just never took the time to notice how cute Callie looked in them. *Damn it Jordan, you're not helping yourself here.*

"I have the notes you're looking for, they're in my office. Bart, please tell Chloe I'll talk to her this afternoon." Callie spoke to the young med student in front of her as he walked away.

"How are you feeling today?" Callie questioned softly. Jordan was dressed nice and tight as usual, but her eyes and her face couldn't hide it. She looked like shit. She was hurting deeply and killing herself because she wouldn't let anyone help her. Callie wanted to hold her. She could still feel her soft wet lips and her warm body.

Jordan tried not to make a big deal out of the

previous days actions. "I'm feeling fine. I need to get those notes and be on my way. I have a lot of things to get done today," she said following Callie to her office. She was unable to stop herself from staring into Callie's eyes one last time as she was handed the file of notes. *I want you so bad, but I can't have you.* She fought off the temptations of kissing the dark-haired woman. She tasted a small amount of her passion once physically and too many other times in her mind. *One time too many*, she thought.

~

Callie laid down on the leather couch next to the window in her office. *Jordan, I am falling so deeply for you. Why can't I have you? The sadness in your eyes is such a horrible sight. I want to hold you close and take that pain away. This ghost you're fighting is killing you. I've been caught in your eyes since the day I met you. I've watched you slowly slip away from reality and past sanity. Damn you, Jordan, let me help you. Please! I need you just as badly as you need me.* She couldn't help the thoughts rumbling through her mind. Watching the detective break down was the worst sight she'd ever seen next to watching her father go through the same thing. It killed him; she wasn't going to let it kill Jordan too.

Callie jumped up from the slight nap she had fallen into when she heard a sound at the door. "It's open," she yelled. *God damn can't someone get some privacy around here?*

"Ah, you're in here. I thought you were gone already," Chloe said.

"I'm sorry. I was busy, I asked Bart to let you know I

would speak with you later today. What's so important that you can't wait until tomorrow to talk to me?"

"I've finished the evaluation you asked for. This, not being my field specialty, has turned out to be one of the most excruciating cases I have ever seen. Here are my notes. I can tell you it wasn't a mutual friend of these girls. He's not someone that they are close to. He's doing this to be vindictive towards someone he knows. He's using a very distinct pattern picking the exact same kind of girl and killing the same way over and over."

"Yeah, I kind of figured that out myself. Thanks for your insight though." *Even though I can't stand you!*

"Sure," Chloe said. "Let me know when I can help again."

"Hey, Chloe, do me a huge favor and please don't mention this to anyone. I don't want anyone knowing I let you take a look at my files on this case. Also, I wouldn't want Detective Denali checking up on me and finding out I talked to you about this. I shouldn't have involved you, but I thank you. You've given me a few ideas to go along with my own. I appreciate it."

"Hey, no problem. If there is anything else I can do for you just let me know."

"If you would excuse me, I think I'm going to call it a night. I have a long day ahead of me tomorrow and wouldn't want to get a late start." Callie followed Chloe out of the room and locked her office door.

~

Jordan woke up in the desk chair at her office. She didn't realize everyone had left already for the evening until she took a lap around the cubical area. She looked down at the small silver Rolex watch on her left arm. *Ten thirty! Damn it how did I fall asleep again?* She quickly retrieved her briefcase from her desk and headed for the elevator. While standing outside of the building she flagged down a cab. *No trolley tonight, I'm too tired to walk down these stairs, much less two blocks uphill to that stop.*

Inside her suite she showered and sat down on the sofa wearing a small T-shirt and a pair of short women's boxer shorts. She poured herself a small glass of scotch. The drink was supposed to help soothe the pain by fading away the graphic images cemented into her head. She could sit there all night and drink herself to her death if she wanted to. Nothing would penetrate the emotions she was drowning in. She finally went to sleep around one a.m.

The five o'clock sounding of the alarm on the nightstand woke Jordan frightfully. As usual she flew out of the bed ready to fire her hand upon anything that moved. She never took her gun out of the holster at night so she wouldn't be able to grab it causing it to go off if she freaked over the alarm.

All she could do was form a hand pistol as her eyes slowly focused on the morning darkness. She went through this every day, fighting the ghosts in her dreams at night, as well as during the day in her thoughts. Sleeping was very hard for her and the alarm always sounded just as she dosed off. Adrenaline was her only fuel and sleep was a luxury that she didn't see much of. Even after she calmed, sitting on the edge of the bed, she couldn't help thinking what it would be like to wake in Callie's arms. *Jordan you can't do this, you'll hurt her too. Callie Marceau, what does it take to let you go? Tell me, please!*

~

After an eager trip to the gym and a shower, Jordan was standing in the captain's office awaiting the moment she knew was going to be a career move for herself along with a life or death decision. One she'd been dreading for roughly three and a half years.

"Captain Osborne?"

"Yes, Jordan, come in," he said.

"Do you remember you telling me to do whatever it takes to catch this guy? Well, I know what it takes. I just need to take some time away from here to get it."

"Jordan, I'm not sure what you're saying, but you're not leaving here again. I can't have that." His voice rose with the blood rushing to his head causing his skin color to change from pink to red.

"Sir, I understand where you're coming from, I really do, but I can't tell you where I have to go. I can only tell you that I will come back here and get him. I just need to go somewhere first. Please trust me on this."

"No. Jordan, I can't let you do this. Something is bothering you and you need to stop running from it. I don't care what you do here! I'm sorry I can't let you leave town."

"Well, if I can't have you behind me this time, that's fine. I work alone and I'll do this alone as well. I have some old business to take care of. I'll be back when I'm finished. When it's all said and done I will return and I will catch this killer."

"Jordan Denali, you can't just leave the city. I'm ordering you to stay here!" The slightly overweight, bald man stood up with his hands planted firmly on the desk like little sausages. The look in his dark beady eyes made Jordan feel bad about leaving, but she had to do what was best for herself.

"Order all you want. The only way I can do this is to go back and settle my unfinished business. I won't be taking any calls from here. I hope you'll give these back to me when I return," Jordan said handing him her issued pistol and badge.

Jordan hated leaving, especially not knowing if she would have a job when this case was over. Catching this guy and stopping the terror that had been ripping through her body and mind was the only thing she could think of, except for Callie. She would have to go without saying a thing to her. She knew the doctor would be hurt again by her actions, but it was hurting her as well. The only way to keep Callie safe was to not involve her at all.

CHAPTER SIX

The airline attendant called for the next flight to board. Jordan jumped up and walked towards the doorway holding her ticket out for the woman to swipe.

She waited for the plane to get into the air before opening her laptop to read some of the notes of the five files. She started preparing to face her ghosts one last time. She was on her way to finish everything that she had left behind and incomplete in her haunted past.

~

Callie called Lance when she noticed the detective wasn't answering any of her phones that morning. "Where did she go? Do you know if she's out of the office for the rest of the day?"

"Callie, she took off. The Captain briefed me a few minutes ago. He said she wasn't acting like herself and she told him she had some unfinished business to take care of and she'd be back when it was complete. I don't know. She turned in her gun and badge. He told me to head up the investigation until she returns. She may not have a job when she comes back, he looked pretty pissed."

"Uh...ok thanks Lance, I'll talk to you later." She hung up the phone hoping Jordan was safe and not in over her head, too deep in her sea of depression to swim for shore. She remembered then that she was waiting for her brother to call with information. He should have something by now; it had been a couple of weeks.

"Eric, it's Callie, I haven't heard anything, I need whatever you can give me as soon as possible please call me back," she said to his voicemail. She hated leaving messages. *God, please let her be ok. I couldn't bear the thought of something happening to her. I should have checked on her. She looked so terrible yesterday. I knew something was wrong and I let it go.*

"Damn it Eric, call me back." Callie wandered around her office, sitting, standing, before pacing outside in the hallway. Two hours went by before the phone at her side finally rang.

"Eric, please tell me you have something," she said.

"Sis, I'm glad to see you're so excited to talk to me since you never..."

"Oh cut the shit Eric, I need this information. She's in trouble."

"Okay calm down. You better watch what you get yourself into Callie. This girl isn't in trouble, she is trouble. Apparently she's from Washington, DC. She went through the academy there and was branded by her colleagues and instructors as the most talented woman to ever leave the academy doors. She's very intelligent, not to mention one of the best sharp shooters of her whole division. Before joining the force she was in the Marines for a brief stroll. There's something medical on her discharge and it looks to be covered up. She was only in there a couple of years."

"Ok so how did she end up in California working for SFPD?" Callie inquired looking for something more.

"Callie, that's all I have. I'll call you in the morning."

Callie pushed the end button on her phone and started pacing again thinking of everything her brother had just told her. No wonder Jordan was so tough. Callie found it appealing thinking of Jordan not only as a Marine but as the bad ass in her academy training. She snickered just a bit. *I bet she was a bitch back there in the academy, look at her now.*

~

The plane landed and Jordan quickly caught a cab to the Double Tree Hotel. She hurriedly checked in and went straight to her king sized bedroom suite. She set up her laptop, inserted an old disk, and began scrolling through the directory. As soon as the file popped up and a name appeared she slammed the computer closed. *Damn it.*

Still not prepared to handle the visit down memory lane, she ordered room service and scanned the wet bar. "What is this shit? There's nothing but cheap ass wine in here." She took her suit jacket off and sat on the chair staring at the muted TV. The image of Callie's smiling face wouldn't leave her mind. Even across the country she could still make Jordan smile. That image came and went between graphic pictures of the man in the file and the reason she had returned. Jordan put her jacket back on.

The lobby had a small bar over in the corner. Jordan took a seat on a stool close to the TV where the news was scrolling.

"Good evening. You seem to be a long way from home. San Francisco, huh? What brings you to DC?" The bartender said looking at her driver's license as he went through his little routine of twenty questions.

"Personal business," she said without looking up.

"Well, what are we drinking tonight?"

"I better keep it simple. Let me have a beer please. Make that in a bottle instead of a glass if you would, thanks," Jordan said.

Jordan's cell phone began to ring on her side. It was Callie. She knew she would be calling as soon as she caught word that Jordan had left. "I guess this as good a time as any to turn you off." She pressed the phone off and put it back in the clip on her side.

"Not taking calls tonight? It must be serious business that has brought you this far."

"Nah, It's nothing. I just had a long flight and I'm tired. I don't feel much like talking." She sat there staring once again into the TV. The sound was mute only to her ears this time. She couldn't concentrate long enough to understand what the news anchors were saying anyway.

Jordan finished her third beer and retreated back to her room. She wanted to call Callie just to hear her sweet voice. She tried harder than anything to push Callie from her mind. Most of her thoughts were merely graphically detailed images of her past, with brief interludes of Callie. Jordan knew Callie would be upset, this time it was best for her to stay away. This would be more painful than anything she could ever imagine. Jordan decided when she first left DC that no one would know of this part of her life, at least as long as she had anything to do with them not knowing. She didn't want to know it herself, much less try to describe it to someone else.

~

Callie made just one call to Jordan, leaving only a short voice mail wishing for her to stay safe and return soon. A few hours later, she crawled into her bed with her dark hair fanning the pillow as a small tear trickled down her left cheek. Eric had only begun to inform her of the detective's tumultuous, secret past. She envisioned the passionately soft kiss they had shared only a few days before. Part of her mind wondered if that was the trigger that set off the whirl wind of emotions she saw spinning out of control in Jordan. She could still feel her warm body up.

The phone next to her bed rang loudly at four a.m. waking her from the sleepless night of tossing and turning.

"Eric, It's about damn time," she said.

"Hey, I don't have to help you. This is serious stuff you're getting involved in here Cal, come on." He was worried about his little sister and knew was a magnet for mystery of any sort.

"Well, get to it. I don't have all day," Callie snapped, agitated and nervous about hearing Eric's news.

"Okay, I told you about her starting the force in DC. Well, she was one of the top detectives for her division there. A little over three years ago she was working day and night on a serial killer case. The records are somewhat fuzzy from there, but it appears the killer found her out and hunted her as a victim. Instead of Jordan, he caught a rookie cop that she was working with, I'm not sure of her name. Anyway, he found this woman and killed her. He got away from Jordan and was caught by another detective six months later. Jordan had left DC by then. She left her career and everything behind and moved to California two days after the brutal murder. I'm assuming that's what happened since she disappeared from their records and appeared in the SFPD records at that time."

"And this guy. Is he still in prison?"

"No, he was given the lethal injection the following year after being caught. Killing an officer sent him straight to the chamber I guess."

"This woman, what did she look like Eric?"

"Um...She was very young with, I think, blond hair, blue eyes, and..."

"Oh no, Jordan. Oh my God." Callie's heart dropped to her stomach. No wonder the detective was killing herself; this guy had to be after Jordan. She knew this was vindictive, she just never knew how far it would go...until now. This also made the PTSD theory about Jordan's behavior much more plausible.

"Callie Marceau, I'm not sure what you have up your sleeve, but, this is major. Don't those dead girls out there fit this description?"

"Hey, Eric, thanks for everything. I really have to go. Wait one other thing, are you sure he's dead?"

"Yeah, I saw his death certificate. Be careful Cal, I'm worried about you."

Callie hung up the phone and ran over to her dresser packing only the necessities. She made a quick call to her boss and long time friend.

"Harvey? It's Callie. Look, I've run in to something serious and I need a few days off. I have..."

"Callie, I need you here, you're heading up this case. Where do you have to go? Can this wait?" he said groggily. "It's the middle of the night."

"No. This is going to help with the case. I just have to go. I'll be back in a few days." He was use to her doing odd ball things over the years. She had been chasing killers since she was old enough to be a part of investigative work.

Three hours later Callie boarded a nonstop flight to DC not knowing what to do or even where to go. *Oh Jordan, please be ok. I can't imagine what you are going through right now. I'll be there soon, hold on. God, why won't she talk to anyone about this fucked up case? I can help her, I know I can.*

~

Jordan awoke when the alarm went off. She wasn't use to the time change, but she went down to the gym anyway. She turned on her laptop when she returned to the room. *I have to read this. I'm going to find your ass this time. I'm tired of chasing your ghost.* She opened the file on the disk still in the computer from the night before.

Weston Garrison, DOB - 9/28/64 DOD - 1/29/10
Cause of Death - Lethal Injection
Victims:
Cindy Holt   - 30 yr old homemaker
Claudine Powers   - 38 yr old church Deacon's wife
Jazmine Daringer - 27 yr old law student
Gim Junitz   - 41 yr old boutique owner, and husband
Karen Junitz   - 39 yr old business assistant and wife
Rachel Doyle   - 23 yr old rookie police officer

He killed his victims by shooting them all point blank in the head. He was caught in the home of an unknowing out of town relative six months after the last shooting.

Jordan closed the file. *What do you have in common with him? How do you know about this? Why now?* There had to be something here that she was missing. She went and turned on the shower as she stripped out of her sweaty work out clothing.

Twenty minutes later, Jordan emerged fresh and clean, wearing a black pants suit and an ocean blue blouse with black and white pin stripes. She was craving a coffee and remembered there was a coffee house on the corner a few blocks away. She put her suit jacket on and walked to the elevator. She hated not having her gun with her, but she turned it in before leaving San Francisco. She carried her small suitcase onto the plane so she didn't have her backup pistol with her either.

~

Callie's cell phone beeped to announce a voice mail. Her brother had called with new information. She quickly grabbed the airplane phone attached to the seat in front of her, hesitating before dialing his number.

He answered on the first ring, "Callie, where are you?" He could hear a small noise in the background and before she could answer him he began to speak in a grizzly voice. "You're in the air! Damn you Callie, what are you doing on a god damn plane?"

"Look, if you've called me to treat me like a child I will just merely hang up. I'm a grown woman and unless you have some new information I suggest you leave me alone."

"Cal, I'm not kidding around here. You always seem to get your ass into the worst predicaments I swear. You're as fucked up as Dad was. Wait, before you hang up I want to tell you to please be careful, wherever you are headed, this is serious."

"Well, are you going to spill it? You're wasting my phone card minutes, Eric."

"Okay, geez, try to be the least bit courteous to your elder here, Cal. Did you know Jordan doesn't have any kind of living establishment in her name, no bills or anything? A few credit cards and a cell phone came up on her credit report but nothing else. I mean no car, apartment, or anything else for that matter. Her mail even goes to a Post Office Box. It's almost as if she doesn't exist. I think she must live in one of your well known high rise hotels. She lives a very secret, sort of seductive life."

"Wow, that's rather interesting information. She gets more mysterious every day. Hey, thanks Eric, I know you're crossing the line by doing this for me. I promise I won't get myself into a mess I can't get out of. Trust me for once." She hung up the phone and stared out of the First Class window to her right. *You can't blame yourself for everything Jordan. You're only human. Let me help you catch this guy.*

~

Jordan walked back to the hotel and the concierge had her rental car waiting out front. She tipped him before opening the door and tossing her briefcase into the passenger seat. She took a short drive out to a two story framed house up on a small hill in what was once a rural neighborhood. The area had turned into a subdivision full of families. This was the site where the first body, Cindy Holt, was found. She was the first person that Weston Garrison killed.

The place looked the same on the outside, except for the condemned sign on the front door and the yard being two feet tall. The small picket fence was still standing and slightly starting to fall apart. The victim's husband had left town and never returned to the heartbroken home he had shared with his wife. Jordan walked around outside and slipped into the kitchen through the back door on the porch. The blood stains and police tape were still there, exactly as they were left close to four years ago. It was like looking into the past inside a perfectly live picture. The tiny hairs on the back of Jordan's neck stood on end as she walked around the house reliving the first time she was there so long ago. This time was different, she was now looking for some reason why he would be back. It was as if this killer from the past had returned from the dead to haunt her.

A half hour later, Jordan went back to the car by the road. She opened a small notebook with all of the addresses and names she had copied off of the computer that morning. Then she drove even further into the outskirts of town to an old wood framed light blue house next to a small white church. This was the second scene in the path of serial crimes Weston Garrison committed. The house was still livable and seemed to be kept up nicely. There was a small car in the driveway on the side. Jordan decided not to go and disturb the new residents. She thought it would be best to leave them at peace. Perhaps they didn't even know about the brutal murder of Claudine Powers that took place in their living room.

Either way, she was going to respect them by not bringing it up. Instead, she drove right past it and back out to the main road.

The third woman, Jazmine Daringer, was killed in her off campus apartment close to the college. It had been a holiday weekend and most of the students had gone out of town. Later in the investigation it came out that Jazmine had befriended Weston only days before her murder. Jordan didn't have a pass to get onto the campus and it wasn't worth scaring the new student that was probably living in that same apartment. She was sure they would have no knowledge of the former occupants or the events that took place in the bedroom there.

~

Callie's plane arrived on schedule. She went straight from luggage claim to the rental car desk. She grabbed a local map and guide book on her way out to the car.

"Hmm, I don't have a god damn clue where to begin. Where are you Jordan?" *Why are you back here?* She drove straight through town to the hotel where she ordered up room service and opened up the map and guide book. She was looking for the nearest library. She would start her search there in the morning since she was exhausted from jet lag and starving due to her lack of appetite for airplane food.

~

Jordan lost track of time during her trip to the next crime scene. The house where Mr. and Mrs. Junitz once lived was torn down by their children a year after the case was closed. It was now just an empty lot full of dirt and overgrown with weeds. They also sold the boutique. The new owners completely renovated it, turning it into a small coffee shop. Jordan went back to the hotel unable to continue on to the last and final crime scene. The terror ripping through her head and the bleeding pain in her heart diverted her attention elsewhere. *I have to be stronger than this.*

Jordan took her clothes off as she walked through the suite. She was completely nude before she made it into the bedroom. She turned on the shower waiting for the hot water before standing under the rippling water trying not to lose herself in the pictures dancing behind her eyelids. One image of him laughing over the bloody body, the next Callie smiling into her eyes. The emotions were tangled together. She could barely feel the difference between past and present as she opened her eyes. After she soaped off and rinsed the conditioner out of her hair she withdrew from the intense heat that was misting off of her body.

She pulled on her soft cotton boxer shorts, as well as a small white T-shirt over her naked breasts. She sat at the little desk in the corner of the room and opened her laptop.

"There has to be something in the police records that indicate what happened while I was gone. I have to find out where they caught him." She said to herself as she searched for over an hour and came up with nothing.

Of course, all of the passwords had changed since she was last there with the police department. She finally fell asleep on the hard bed in the next room. In her sleep, her mind kept taking her back to that evening she shared with the Callie in her arms, the passionate kiss played over and over. She could almost feel the warmth of Callie's body against her own.

CHAPTER SEVEN

Five a.m. the alarm went off as usual. Jordan was completely wrapped in the sheets and lying diagonally across the bed. The comforter had fallen to the floor. She'd been tossing and turning all night, sleeping only a few hours at a time. She quickly changed into her work out clothes and grabbed her sneakers as she tore through the hotel room door and down to the gym.

An hour later, she returned soaked in sweat with her muscles still twitching from the vigorous workout. She showered and wrote a few scribbles in the notebook before dressing in a charcoal gray pants suit and white blouse.

She drove straight to the police station and the office she had gone to everyday for most of her career. It was also the same office she hadn't seen since her life fell apart. A few officers as well as detectives turned around as she walked through the door. It was unusual for someone they didn't know to come up to their department.

"Hi, I would like to speak with Captain Stewart. Is he in his office?" Jordan hadn't really seen any familiar faces, especially not the one at the desk in front of her. This kid was young and had to be a rookie since he left her standing there while he walked back to his Sergeant's desk. They returned together.

"Hi, I'm Sergeant Milton, is there something I can do

for you, Ma'am?" He was shorter than she was, with a slight build and cropped, military cut, brown hair.

"I'm a former employee here and I would like to speak with Captain Stewart concerning some old business. My name is Jordan Denali. If you would please tell him I'm here that would be great," she said as she began to quietly lose her composure. She wasn't use to dealing with the low men on the totem pole. She was well known in that building at one time. That same notorious image had not followed her to California, but it was definitely on the rise there, especially with this case at hand.

The Sergeant walked into the Captain's office and immediately they both came out together. "Jordan! It's been a long time," The white haired man said. He came right up to her with his arms out. She hugged him and returned the excited greeting. He had always treated her like a daughter and she never asked why. She wasn't sure if she wanted to know the reason. "Please, come on into my office. How are you? What brings you back here?" As he shut the door, Jordan sat in the leather chair in front of the large wooden desk.

"Yes it has been a long time, Sir. Almost four years to be exact. I'm actually here on business. I never thought I'd be coming back here, but..."

As he sat down in his chair he looked her square in the face. "How are you doing, Jordan? You didn't answer me and you know you can't ignore the question. You don't look much better than you did the day you walked out of here. I was worried about you. Hell, we all were. I hear you're doing pretty good out in California if I remember correctly."

"Yes, Sir. I'm a Lieutenant Detective for the San

Francisco Police Department. I've returned because I'm in need of some information. I'm working on a case that an old file might help me solve..."

"Yes, go on. You still haven't told me what I want to hear," he said.

She trembled as she spoke. "I need to see the Garrison file, Sir."

"Oh, Jordan, I don't think that's a good idea. Look at you, it's been four years. You need to let it go. We caught his ass and he's now in hell paying his debt. It's over. It's been over for a long time," he sighed.

"I can't. It's not about me this time. I have a serious case on my hands and I believe there is something in this file that can help me with it. I wasn't here for the end. Those details may hold the key to unlocking this mess I'm dealing with back home. I need you to do this for me, Captain Stewart. You know this will be the one and only time I ever ask to see that file. As far as I'm concerned, he can rot in hell. I swear to you, if it wasn't serious or I didn't think it would be useful, you and I both know I would not be here right now," she pleaded.

"I just don't think it's healthy for you, Jordan. I can look at you right now and see it in your eyes, you're not over it. You're not over her."

"This has nothing to do with...with her. I'm telling you I need the information on him."

"Jordan he's dead, it's over." He stood up with his palms flat on the desk looking straight at her eyes.

"No it's not. I know he's dead, but his...look I need this information. If you won't help me, well I guess I'll have to get it another way. I think someone is copying Garrison's work and taunting me with it. Innocent people are dying, Stewart, damn it I can't stop this guy."

"Calm down Jordan. Are you sure it's a copycat?"

"It's either that or we got the wrong guy. Maybe he had an accomplice. I don't know. Captain Stewart, bodies that look like Rachel are popping up all over the god damn city," Jordan ran her hand through her hair.

He watched the frustration cross Jordan's face. In the years that he had known her he had never seen her wound this tight. "I'll get you access to the file, but under one condition, you have to be in and out of it. I mean it. I'm not supposed to let you look at any of our files, you're gone now. You walked, better yet, ran out of here a long time ago. Make it quick and promise me this isn't about her. You have to move on, Jordan, you just have to. You're killing yourself over something you couldn't control."

"I understand. I need to make this fast anyway. I have some other business to take care of today."

"I'll be right back with it. Stay in here."

She was still shaking, hoping he didn't notice her hands trembling in her lap, and the beads of sweat along her hairline around the back of her neck as he walked out of the door. He returned a few minutes later with a thick manila folder full of papers, pictures, and every bit of detailed information.

"Here, I'll leave you alone for a few minutes. Want some coffee or something?"

"Uh, no, I'm fine thanks," she said waiting for him to leave so she could open the file.

He left the room and she opened the folder. Laying on top of the notes and documents was the picture that she'd seen so many nights in her head and over and over again behind her lids every time they closed. She gasped as she turned the page. *Oh god, I...I can't do this.*

She fought back tears as she read the profile of the guy that had ruined her life. In her mind, yes he had died, but he had taken a piece of her with him. She flipped all of the pictures of him and his victims over so that she didn't have to see her.

At the end of the thick booklet of papers was the indictment information. She pulled out her notepad and began writing chicken scratch notes of Weston Garrison's final days on the run, as well as his time on death row. He was finally apprehended in the house of his cousin, Andrew Dexon. That name didn't sound familiar at all to Jordan. She wrote everything down as fast as she could. The captain returned quickly, just as he said he would.

"Did you find what you were looking for? I'm curious to know what it was," he said.

"Um...well, I didn't quite find it, but that's ok. Captain, look thanks for everything you've done for me. I mean the recommendation, the support...everything. I ..."

"Somehow, Jordan, I understand a small part of you, maybe that's why I didn't stop you when you left. You're a very talented woman. I hate to see your skills wasted. I'm glad I could be of assistance to you."

Jordan stood up shaking his hand and walked towards the door. She opened her mouth to speak, but the words wouldn't come out. He understood what she was trying to say though.

"Go on, get outta here. Catch your guy and, Jordan, take care of yourself."

She walked out of the office and turned towards the Sergeant and the other detectives in the room before walking through the cubical desks to the main entrance. The place really hadn't changed much except for the wreath with a yellow ribbon and a fallen officer's name on it. Seeing that brought a small tear to Jordan's eye as she exited the building.

~

Callie awoke around eight a.m. and showered before heading out of the hotel to the library that was located a few blocks away. She showed her ID to gain access to the microfiche films as she sat in front of the newspaper chronicles and news videos. She looked up serial killer information as well as Jordan's name through the months of the year 2009.

Callie finally found the pages and news video footage she was looking for. She sat there for two hours writing notes as she read of the horrifying serial crimes that were committed in the case Jordan had been working on. The papers mentioned a young woman named Rachel Doyle, a Rookie Officer working with the Homicide Division who would turn out to be the killer's last victim. *Oh Jordan, I'm so sorry. I'm so...so sorry.*

She wiped away a few small tears streaming down her right cheek as she saw the brief footage of Rachel in the news video. She was beautiful, shoulder length blond hair and light gray, almost baby blue eyes. She was just a bit shorter than Jordan as far as she could tell from the news videos that had them talking together in a press conference in the first few stages of the investigation.

When she was finished with all of her notes she read over the obituary on Rachel before she turned everything off. She knew somehow Jordan was deeply involved in the case back in California, not only emotionally, but also physically. It was clear now after reading the information and seeing the pictures, that this new killer knew most of

Jordan's past and was haunting her with it. No wonder Jordan was so dark all of the time. The secrets of her life were forbidden, even to her. *I'll find you, Jordan, I don't know what to say to you but I'll find you. Damn, Callie, you always manage get yourself into the worst predicaments.*

~

Jordan drove the rental car through the tall iron gates and parked along the curb in the back. She had a small red rose in her right hand as she stepped out and walked through the low cut grass stopping in front of a small marble head stone that read: Washington DC Police Officer, Rachel Leigh Doyle, October 10, 1986 to June 18, 2009. 'She was a brave young woman who gave her life in the line of duty. She will be truly missed.'

As Jordan read the inscription tears that had filled her eyes the moment she pulled into the cemetery began to flow down her cheeks like a water fall. When she set the rose down on the stone, she let out a small gasp losing the breath in her lungs and dropping to her knees. She cried out all of the pain that she had held in for the past four years. "Oh Rachel, I'm so sorry. I...this should be me here. Damn you, Lord," She began screaming. "Damn you. Why? Why her? Why did you take her away? Why? You let that son of bitch take her from me. Why, I don't understand, God...why?"

She threw her hands up in the air. Her head was pounding, on fire from the pressure and the excruciating pain coming from her body.

"Rachel, I'm so sorry I walked away from you. I was supposed to protect you. Instead, I failed you." The tears were still running down her burning red face and flowing onto her shirt that was soaking with sweat and tears. "I miss you so much. If I could only turn the time around, I would never have left you alone. I'm so…so sorry."

Jordan cradled her face with her hands whimpering as the agony poured from her heart.

Jordan wailed, crying out a small moan that came from deep inside her body. She had never mourned the death of her co-worker, friend, and most of all, lover. Instead, she ran three-thousand miles away from everything and pushed it all away deep down inside and into the back of her mind. She was so far gone in the screaming and crying fit to hear the footsteps coming up behind her.

Callie stood back watching this woman in front of her break down like she was bleeding to death, tearing and screaming. Jordan was beyond recognition, except for her short hair and her attire. Callie wanted to hold her and couldn't resist the aching feeling any longer.

She squatted behind the kneeling woman that was slumped over in front of the marble stone. Callie put her hands on Jordan's shoulders and Jordan jumped, snatching herself away from the dark-haired woman's touch as she turned around. Jordan couldn't believe her eyes. Callie held back the tears that her eyes were swimming in.

Jordan looked like her heart was being ripped out. Her face was red and soaked with tears and her eyes were black instead of the normal sapphire blue. Neither woman spoke until Jordan slowly opened her mouth, still crying.

"What?" She couldn't stop the sobbing. "What…are you doing here? Why are you here?" Jordan said.

Callie didn't know what to say to the woman sitting

in front of her on the ground.

"Please leave me alone. I've...I've told you before, this has noth..." Jordan was choking on the tears now. "Nothing...to do with you. Please go."

Callie leaned over and put her arms around Jordan tightly pulling the detective against her. Jordan fought it only for a second and gave in to the soft comforting arms.

Callie could feel Jordan trembling, gasping for air as she sat there weeping.

She didn't say anything, she just sat there holding Jordan in her arms wishing for the pain to go away. She pressed her lips lightly to Jordan's forehead. Jordan's face was tucked up against Callie's neck. She could feel the heat coming from Jordan's face and the warm wet tears that were now dripping onto her shoulder. They sat there for a while with Callie holding her while she grieved for the first time over the terrible loss that she'd suffered. She cried until she was out of tears.

After thirty minutes, Jordan leaned away from Callie as she began vomiting from the devastating stress of her anguish. She turned back towards the woman and looked up at her.

"Do you think you could maybe give me a minute alone here?"

Callie nodded and brushed her lips across the top of Jordan's head as she stood up. She knew the detective needed time to regain her composure. She stepped back and walked towards the two parked cars.

"Rachel..." A small tear trickled down Jordan's already soaked cheek. "I'm so sorry. I'll never be the same, not without you. If I had only listened to you. I should've been there, not you." The tears started flowing again. "I'll never let you go, Rachel. I'm so sorry, I could

106

never ask for your forgiveness. I...I love you Rachel. I've never stopped. I will always love you."

All of a sudden the hair on the back of her neck stood up as she looked over at Callie leaning against her rental car. "What are you trying to tell me Rachel? I need you. I know I don't deserve your help, but I don't know how to stop him before he does this again." She began to feel a small amount of the pressure lifting from her chest as the wind blew harder. "Good bye, Rachel," Jordan said as she kissed her fingers and placed them on the cold stone before sanding up. She turned wiping the tears from her face once more as she walked towards Callie.

"I can't leave you alone. You're in no condition to even drive yourself," Callie said.

"I...I'm fine Callie. I just need...some time."

"There comes a time, Jordan, when it's okay to not be so tough. Please, let me help you. Let me in." Callie put her arms around the sobbing woman and Jordan slightly pulled away, but fell back into the warm embrace. Their bodies fit tightly together.

"I need to get out of here," Jordan said backing away from Callie and separating them. She grabbed the keys out of her pocket and turned towards her rental car.

"Okay, at least let me follow you to your hotel. I have to make sure you're safe. I'll worry if I don't."

"Fine, I'm staying at the Double Tree. It's not too far from here," Jordan said.

Fifteen minutes later they pulled up at the hotel. Callie parallel parked by the curb and Jordan handed her keys to the valet at the front door. Callie walked across the street and met up with Jordan going into the main entrance. They stepped into the elevator and Jordan kept silent during the ride up and the short walk down the hall to her suite.

She motioned for Callie to walk in front of her into the room. Callie moved inside and sat on the small tan colored love seat while Jordan took her suit jacket off laying it on the back of the desk chair. She walked into the bedroom and sat on the edge of the bed with her head in her hands.

Callie decided not to follow Jordan into the bedroom figuring she needed some space to get her thoughts together, so she turned the TV on and stared at the wall. Her mind was recalling the event that had just unfolded in front of her less than an hour ago. *My god, how has she been able to handle this? She's so strong.*

Jordan went into the bathroom and splashed water on her face. "Damn, I look like shit," she said to the mirror. She quickly changed into more comfortable clothes and gargled some mouthwash to get the terrible taste out of her mouth before going out to sit on the couch.

"Uh...are um...are you hungry?" Jordan wasn't sure what to say to Callie since she was feeling rather nervous and very embarrassed.

"Yeah, a little." Callie answered back. She didn't care what they did. She just wanted to be close to Jordan. She really wanted to hold her. The feeling of having Jordan in her arms wouldn't go away.

"Well, this place has a decent room service menu. I can call down for an early dinner if you want."

"That'd be great."

~

Callie had learned most of the facts, but she wanted to hear the story. There was definitely more to Jordan's painful past than she could have ever imagined. She watched Jordan as she lay on the couch sleeping. Callie put a small blanket over her and went into the bedroom and sat down on the bed. It was late and she had decided to stay the night, not wanting to leave Jordan to face the trauma alone.

Two hours later, she heard Jordan screaming at the top of her lungs and tearing at the blanket that was wrapped around her. She ran right to Jordan's side on the couch and couldn't believe the sight. Jordan's eyes were black and the tears had returned. She was screaming, "No! No! God No! Please!"

"Jordan, it's Callie," she said calmly. Sitting on the edge of the couch she put her arms around Jordan pulling her tightly against her body. Jordan's face was buried against Callie's neck as she gently rocked back and forth trying to sooth the pain of the woman in her arms. "It's ok. I'm here now. It's ok Jordan."

She finally got her quieted down. Jordan was still shaking just as she had been early that day on her knees at the cemetery.

"I'm here if you want to talk, Jordan. Maybe that will help. You can let me in. I won't hurt you."

Jordan sat there for a while letting Callie hold her. She finally started to calm down.

"It's not that easy, Callie, I..." Jordan stumbled over her words. She wasn't ready to let Callie hear the heartbreaking story of her past.

"I'll be here as long as you need me to be. I understand."

They sat in silence. Callie concentrated on Jordan's heart beating against her chest.

"You should go get into your bed, Jordan. I'll take

the couch."

"I couldn't do that to you, Callie."

"No, please. It's ok," Callie insisted.

"Are you sure? I mean it's quite alright with me if you take the bed."

"No, don't be silly, I'll be fine out here. I have you to protect me, don't I?"

Jordan looked up with sad eyes that had now turned to a deep dark blue instead of the unforgiving blackness that filled them before.

"I'm not a good protector, Callie. You'll get hurt. I can't protect you from..."

"Hey now, I was kidding with you. Go get in your bed, I'll see you when the sun comes up."

~

Callie woke up at six and Jordan was gone. Her stuff was still there but she had left the room. Callie knew she didn't go far since she had left her briefcase and laptop in the table.

The door opened when Callie walked back into the living area. The detective walked in wearing gym clothes and sneakers. She was still feeling slightly nervous and a little ashamed at what Callie had seen. No one ever saw Jordan grieve, not even her family.

"Hey, you're up early."

"Yeah, I was looking for you," Callie said.

"I get up at five everyday and go to the gym for an hour. I'm sorry I..."

"No, it's ok. I remember you doing that when we were in Florida. I just didn't think you would be feeling up to it today."

"Truthfully, I didn't. Not at all, but I had to. It keeps me going. Anyway, I...uh...I'm not very good with this kind of thing...but I just wanted to say..."

"It's ok, Jordan. I know," Callie said looking up at the ocean blue eyes staring back at her. She smiled softly before Jordan went into the bedroom to shower.

They left the room together heading down to check out in the lobby. Jordan realized that Callie probably wasn't ready since she had stayed all night with her.

"Where were you staying?" Jordan asked.

"I'm at the hotel up the street."

"Alright, well you should probably go pack while I finish up here. We can take your rental to the airport."

"That sounds good. I have to shower."

~

Jordan already had her return flight scheduled and Callie had an open ticket so they went straight to the ticket counter. They were able to get seats together on the earlier flight that was already boarding. They rushed through security and jumped in line for First Class boarding. The plane ride was long and the food was terrible. Neither woman ate. Jordan did a lot of writing on her laptop into the file notes while Callie stared out the window until she fell asleep. Jordan watched her huddled in the corner with her eyes closed. *I'm sorry you had to see that Callie. I wish you weren't there, but in a small way, I'm glad you were. I know you were probably up all night. Thank you.*

Back on the ground they shared a cab that dropped them off at there separate homes. Before parting, Jordan went to shake Callie's hand and Callie pulled her into her arms, holding her one last time. She couldn't resist the urge to feel that tight warm body against her own.

Jordan didn't want to let go. She needed Callie; this woman was the only thing that made her feel alive again. Through the whole night as well as the whole trip back, no one talked about the ordeal that had taken place the day before. She knew Callie wanted to know why she broke down in the cemetery and what caused her to hurt that deeply. There was so much more to the story. She wasn't sure if she could ever tell it. In the back of her mind, Jordan wondered how and why Callie had found her. She decided not to mention it at all. She didn't want to dredge the pain back up. It was still only lingering just below the surface.

Jordan asked Callie not to let anyone know she was back. Callie agreed that Jordan needed a day or two to get herself back together. She offered to stay and help her, but Jordan refused. She believed it was better for her to be alone. She had already put the woman through too much as it was.

~

For the next twenty-four hours Jordan sat around her suite, changing once from a short silk robe to a pair of cotton shorts and a tank top before she read over her notes and files. She poured herself a glass of scotch from the crystal decanter on the bar and went back to the couch.

As she sat their sipping her drink, she couldn't quite make the connection between the Bay City Killer and Garrison. A copy cat wouldn't know this much, not about her personally. No this had to be someone that knew him, as well as her past with Rachel, or at least the fact that they were working together and she was one of his victims. *Who are you, what do you want with me?*

On top of dealing with a serial killer haunting her, she also had the pressure of the newfound feelings for Callie that she had somehow acquired over the past few months. It didn't matter how far she pushed them, they returned immediately, ten times stronger than before. *Damn you, I can't do this, not now…not ever.*

CHAPTER EIGHT

Callie thought about calling Jordan, but she knew deep down the call would only fuel the burning desire to touch her. Still, she had to believe she'd ignited some sort of spark while they were together in DC. Jordan did in fact give in and let Callie hold her. *Was she feeling the same passion that I felt against her body, or was I merely a safe haven until the pain was gone? Jordan, if you would only talk to me, damn it let me in.*

~

Jordan crawled out of bed heading straight for the gym. She needed a wakeup call since she had practically just fallen asleep. After the workout, she took a shower and headed out the door to start her day when she saw Garrison's face flash before her eyes followed by Rachel's bloody body. She stopped walking and backed against the building for support. The picture in her mind quickly morphed Rachel's body into Callie's. Jordan's heart raced. *Not now. Please I can't concentrate like this. Not with Callie in those pictures. I have to stop thinking about her, damn it, it's killing me to not be near her.*

She regained her composure and flagged down a cab instead of hurrying down to the trolley stop.

"City Hall building, please," she said to the driver.

She arrived in front of the large building and paid the

fare.

"Damn, I never called in to let Osborne know I was back. Shit," she said. *Hope I still have a job when I walk through this door.*

She rode the elevator up to the third floor and walked into the Homicide Division. Lance caught a glimpse of her across the room from his cubical desk. Not believing his eyes, he did a double take as Jordan walked right by him on her way to the Captain's office. She knocked and entered the small room.

"I see you have returned. Is this a good decision or a bad decision, Lieutenant? We never did discuss further employment for you when you handed me your gun and badge," he said. His was sitting as his desk with his hands flat on the desk.

"Well Sir, that's why I..."

"I know why you're here, Jordan. That's not what I'm asking. Are you still employed at this office?"

"At this present time, Sir, yes. I have not seen nor have I signed a termination document and I have not turned in my resignation. I do believe that means I'm still on the payroll. I would like to ask your permission to continue to be a part of this office and this team. I know what I..."

"Team? Jordan, do you know what a team is?" His voice began to rise a notch or two."I don't believe you do."

"Sir, with all due respect, may I please explain what's going on?" she said. Playing his game was only pissing her off.

"Ok, but I'm warning you, Lieutenant Denali, you're on paper thin ice with me right now."

She wasn't sure if his face was turning red or if it was

115

her eyes making him appear that way.

"Captain Osborne, I know I shouldn't have left, but I had to take care of a personal matter that came up unexpectedly. I've learned a few things about myself, as well as this case."

"Jordan, it's like this..."

"I want to finish what I have to say."

"Go on," he said.

"I know I haven't been the best of friends with anyone here, but that's not the issue. You and I both know I can catch this guy. I believe I may have some insight as to who he is. Whether or not I spend quality time with these desk jockeys you have outside doesn't mean I can't do my job. I'm not tooting my own horn here. I know I can be replaced as a person, but my intelligence and my skills have gotten me into the situation that I'm in with this case. I didn't ask for it. If I do recall, I refused and you threw it up in my face that I'm the veteran around here. If I want to continue to be a part of this division and receive a paycheck then I had better take this assignment.

"I didn't mean to run out on anyone. I did what was best for me at the time. I know how to solve this case. I just have to solve it my way. If that is too much of a problem, well then, you can keep my badge and my issued weapon. I know what I did wasn't right. I will take whatever action you toss at me. I only did what I had to do to figure out this guy's pattern. It's the only way I can stop him."

"Well, Jordan, I do believe you have yourself a set of steel balls. Your ego is about to swallow us both. I'm not going to say I understand, because I don't. I'm also not going to keep your badge or your gun. Instead, I'm going to send you back out there to nail this bastard. When it's all over with I will decide what to do with you. As of right now you're pending suspension when this case is solved." He stood up with his palms still flat on the desk. His eyes were small and beady like a stuffed animal. "That will be all, Lieutenant. I hope to hear an update on this case as soon as it becomes available."

She practically ran to her office and slammed the door behind her. "Jordan, what the fuck are you thinking? Do you really want to lose your career?" *Okay, you can't think about this or that right now. There is a killer on the loose and for some fucked up reason he's tormenting you. Get your ass together and go find him.*

~

Callie stepped from the elevator. She passed by Chloe and Bart gossiping in the hallway. *Don't you guys have anything better to do?* She bypassed her office and went into the Chief Medical Examiner's office. Harvey McCormick was sitting behind his large wooden desk reading files and signing documents as usual.

"Callie, I'm glad to see you've returned. I'm also glad to inform you that thankfully nothing came up while you were gone. You got lucky this time. I just don't know how much more of this I can take. I didn't know your dad, but I hope one day you can let it all go. Sometimes, things just happen."

"I know. Harvey, listen this had nothing to do with my father, please believe me. It's over, I'm back now, and everything is...well...not much has changed. Still, I had to do it and now I'm back. I can't promise you I won't have to go away again. I can only tell you I will try my best not to."

117

"It seems like you may be trying to compromise. I don't accept it. When the Assistant D.A. is here snooping around and my lead on this case is off chasing ghosts, god knows where, this whole office looks bad. Luckily, you were sick for a few days. I'm telling you Dr. Marceau, no more! You're either here doing your god damn job or you're gone!"

Callie had known Harvey the whole five years that she'd been a Medical Examiner. He was one of the people she worked with right out of college. Friend or not, he was pissed. This time she crossed the line.

"Okay, I understand. I..."

"Callie, please, just go do some work. I don't have time to discuss this any further."

She walked out of the room and back down the hall to her own office. Sitting down in the small leather chair, she opened her notes from the trip. She wondered if she was going to see Jordan any time soon. Her body definitely wanted to see Jordan again. Just thinking of the detective made Callie's legs flutter. *God I have to stop thinking about her. She constantly has my head spinning.*

~

Jordan sat at her desk with her suit jacket off scanning through the files and her hand written notes going through every piece of information on the case. One by one she began putting together pieces of the puzzle behind the killings. *You pick out girls that resemble Rachel since you know that will hit home with me. You beat them to kill them, probably out of anger. Then, you cut them to make your marks for your handy work. After they're dead, you rape them because you know that will only make my pain worse. That's the fun part of the game for you. In your mind you're raping her, making Rachel suffer. Finally, you shoot them the same way he did, in honor of him.* "You sick twisted son of a bitch!"

She snatched her cell phone off of her side and pushed the number two for speed dial.

"Williams."

"Lance, it's Jordan, I want you to round up Grant, Ingram, and Conrad and meet me in the conference room in one hour."

"Yes, Ma'am," he said frowning as he stared towards her closed office door.

"Oh and Lance, keep this between us. No one else knows." She ended the call without hearing his answer and threw her files and laptop back into her briefcase. She quickly put her jacket on and left her office. She noticed Lance was already gone from his cubical desk when she walked towards the elevator.

~

Outside of the building, the sky was bright blue; the air was crisp and warm. No humidity was a nice thing to have in the middle of July. She turned and proceeded down the sidewalk to the coffee shop on the corner. Jordan bumped into Callie walking out of the door of the coffee shop as she was walking in.

"Good afternoon, Doctor," Jordan said. She hadn't seen nor spoken to Callie since the breakdown in DC.

"Hello there, Detective, what brings you out of the office today?"

"Just getting a jump start on what is turning out to be

a long day," Jordan said.

"Yes, it seems to have turned out that way for me as well." Callie hated putting on the professional front outside of their offices. She wanted to hold Jordan and ask her how she was feeling. The pain was definitely still lingering on the surface.

"I guess I better get my coffee and be on my way. I'm sure you're just as busy as I am." Jordan stumbled over her words. Looking at Callie always caused butterflies in her stomach.

"Yes, I have a pile of paperwork to complete. Would you like to go have a drink with me later?" Callie's heart stopped as she waited for the answer. She held her breath, biting her lower lip nervously.

"I'm sorry. I'm tied up all evening I don't know when I'll get out of the office. I have a lot of loose ends to tie up from being gone," Jordan said. She wanted to say yes. Her heart was screaming yes, but her mind was telling her to run as fast as she could.

"Okay, some other time then," Callie said walking away and trying to hide the sad look on her face. She knew something was up with Jordan. She could see it flaring in her dark blue eyes.

~

Jordan walked into the square shaped conference room. Ten leather chairs surrounded a wooden, rectangle shaped table. She took her seat at the head of the table, setting a manila folder and her coffee cup down in front of her. Lance sat on one side of her with Patrol Sergeant Jeremy Conrad on his right. He was a tall, white man with short, military cut blond hair. The other two men at the table sat on her left side. They were homicide detectives, Robert Grant, a tall and skinny, dark-haired man and his partner Vincent Ingram, a short, well-built, black man.

Jordan felt four sets of eyes on her as she opened the folder and closed it again. Most of the men in the department knew who she was. They were intimated by her. Mostly because she could shoot them between the eyes with her eyes closed, but also because she was so introverted. No one knew how to approach her or talk to her for that matter.

"The reason I have asked all of you here is to discuss our current situation. Everyone knows of the Bay City Killer and his victims. I've arranged a plan of surveillance hoping we can catch him at his next drop off point. This calls for some undercover work that some or all of you may not be familiar with. I do not want anyone else to know of this. I will personally advise the captain of every move we make. It's my rules or you don't play at all. Are we all clear?" she said watching each man nod in her direction.

"Okay, then here it is." She opened the file containing two pictures as well as two drawings in it with some hand written notes on the side. "We're going to stake out the Golden Gate Bridge as well as the Bay Bridge."

"Lieutenant, what about the patrol officers that have been running the detail around the crime scenes?" Grant asked.

"Wait a second, I'll get to that. Let me explain the details and then I'll answer your questions. Conrad, you need to hand-pick three patrol officers that you trust and pull the rest of the detail off the bridges. You need to put one of them on each end of each bridge including yourself at the fourth location, but make sure they are far enough away to be out of sight. You also need someone back here that can run plates for us as we call them in. We will need you guys as backup if we spot him. We won't have cars anywhere near us so your guys may have to chase him down.

"Grant, you and Ingram will be on opposite ends of the Bay Bridge and Williams and myself will be on opposite ends of the Golden Gate Bridge. The key here is stay hidden and out of sight. If he sees any of us he will abort the site and we will miss probably our only chance to catch him. I'm hoping he is sloppy and will continue the same pattern of dumping women over the bridge.

"We will all be wired with mics and ear pieces so that we can remain in constant contact. I will have access on two frequencies so that I can speak to all of you on one channel and communicate back here at the station on the other.

"We'll start tonight. He's been dumping the bodies approximately between twelve and two a.m. so we'll arrive on scene at eleven. Everyone will remain in their positions until three. If you see anything suspicious, such as the same vehicle driving back and forth, a vehicle stopped, anyone walking along, or something that is out of the ordinary I want to know about it. You're not going to be able to see each other so you'll have to rely on radio communication. Use your binoculars to read license plates and check out drivers as cars pass by. I want a description of anything you see that looks odd. Even if it looks normal I want you to think of it as being him, or his next victim. I'll transmit everything back here so they can run the plate numbers.

"I know I'm probably the only one here who has had any experience with this type of work, but if it's done right we may get a lucky break. Are there any questions?" She closed the folder, placing her hands on top of the file with her fingers locked together.

"What if he spots us and doesn't go through with it?" Ingram said.

"That's a chance we are going to have to take. If you position yourselves out of sight, you more than likely will not be seen by anyone. It's going to be dark and you all need to dress in black. Make sure there is no writing on your shirts. If you don't have any fatigue style pants that fit you have time to go get a pair at the uniform store. Give the captain your receipt. Also, make sure you are wearing your bullet proof vest and have your service weapon and a backup.

"If you see someone stop their vehicle or walking around out there, radio me and I'll give the orders. No one is to approach him alone or without my orders." She looked down at her watch, it was already four. You can go for the day. Get some sleep, eat, and be ready to go tonight." *This has to work. Come on you asshole, I'm ready for you.*

Jordan walked into the captain's office and shut the door before taking a seat in the chair across from the desk. From the way he glared at the woman sitting in front of him, he was obviously still pissed at her.

"What brings you back here?" he said.

"I'm updating you on our situation. I have an arrangement with an undercover team to observe the bridges starting tonight," she said.

"Do you think that's a wise decision?" He wasn't sure he liked the idea of going after this guy with minimal force.

"Yes, I believe we will either get him or get very close to him. I have Grant and Ingram, Williams and myself. Conrad will have someone here in the office running plates and he will be in the field heading the back up team."

"I'm confident you will do fine, Jordan. This is what you're good at. I believe you're the best one in this building to have going face to face with this S.O.B., but safety is a our number one concern. These men aren't..."

"Sir, I know these men weren't trained the same way I was. I completely understand that. I have simply asked them to volunteer for the assignment. They were eager to get started, so I went forward. No one else in this building knows and it will stay that way. I have plenty of coverage on and off the field."

"I'm behind you on this. Do what you have to do to catch his ass. I mean it, Jordan, dead or alive! What do you need from me?"

"We will meet up here tonight at ten. We're going to need to be wired with mics and ear pieces and I need to be able to use two frequencies so I can be in contact with whoever is here running the plates."

"Okay, I'll have the equipment ready for you by nine. I'll stay back here tonight with Conrad's officer that way I can be in contact with everyone. Be careful, Jordan. This guy is serious and he's dangerous."

"Yes, Sir, I know." *And he has a hard on for me, for some fucked up reason that I can't seem to figure out.*

~

Lance went up to the fifth floor to see if Chloe was

in her office. He was supposed to give her a folder that pertained to another case and had forgotten with all of the excitement over the night operation. He ran into Callie in the hallway when he stepped from the elevator.

"Hi, Callie, how are you?"

"Hello Lance, what brings you up here?" She could see him staring directly at her breasts.

"Oh, I forgot to leave something with Chloe earlier and I'm headed out for the day," he said.

"Have a hot date? You seem to be in a rush?"

"No date, I'm working all night," he said.

"All night, what's going on?"

"Jordan has a few of us working tonight with her."

Callie was confused. Jordan never worked with anyone, especially not the half ass goons in her office. "So, what does the old battle axe have you guys doing?"

"Not much, just sort of pretending to be peeping toms." He smiled, laughing slightly.

"Who are you spying on?" Callie asked. Her blood pressure rose a few notches. If Jordan was up to something on the case she wanted to know about it.

"I can't tell you. I'm not even supposed to say what I've already said. Jordan would mop the floor with my head if she knew I was even talking to you."

"Yeah, she can be a hard ass to work with sometimes. Well, have fun."

Lance walked down the hall and Callie went to her office. *I know she's up to something. Damn her! I want to be there when they catch him. Where are you going, Jordan? It has to be serious if you called in the cavalry.*

~

Jordan finally made it back to her place. "There is no way I can sleep and I'm so fucking tired," she said to the empty room pouring herself a calming glass of scotch. "One relaxing glass to cool my nerves and then I'll do some more work," she promised herself. *If I don't calm down I'm going to be delusional out there. Come on, regain your control. He can't win if you don't let him. It wouldn't be so bad if the damn hallucinations and nightmares would go away. My head doesn't know day from night anymore.*

It was nine-thirty p.m. before Jordan realized it. She quickly dressed in faded blue jeans, a white polo shirt, and black boots. She was casual since she planned to change at the office anyway. She carried a small black gym bag that held her service issued forty-five caliber automatic and the 9mm she used as a backup. Her black Kevlar vest and fatigue clothes were also in the bag.

She took a cab since she didn't want to be on the trolley carrying all of her gear. The ride was short and quiet. She sat nervously thinking about how she hadn't done any kind of field work since the night Rachel was killed. The further she pushed the memory away, the quicker it bounced right back. She swore she wouldn't do this kind of detail again. If she could only make herself believe she didn't have to do it, then she wouldn't be doing it.

Jordan arrived just before ten and quickly changed clothes before walking into the conference room. The Captain was talking to Conrad who was standing across from him by the table. Lance walked in behind her with Grant and Ingram following him. The Captain let her have the floor as he went back to his office to call and let his wife know he would be home late that evening. All four of the guys were looking oddly at her. None of them had ever seen her outside of the neatly pressed suits she donned every day. She had never seen them dressed in fatigues either, but then again she never really paid them much attention to begin with.

"We should have all of our equipment in the conference room."

"The captain locked everything in there so no one would notice it," Conrad said.

"Come on, I have keys to the room," she said.

Everyone followed her down the hall as she removed the keys from her pocket and stepped inside.

"Here we go. Williams, here is your radio and ear piece. Place it into your ear with the wired antenna behind your ear. Push the tiny button on the outside to transmit. Grant, Ingram, here you go. Look at the way Lance has his and put yours the same way. Conrad, here's yours too. Now, I want everyone to separate on different areas of this floor so you can't be heard unless you transmit."

Jordan went into her office and closed the door. *Well, here we go.* She pushed the button in her ear. "Williams, do you copy?"

"Loud and clear," Lance said.

"Grant, do you copy?"

"I'm here," Grant said.

"Ingram, do you copy?"

"This thing sounds better than my cell phone," Ingram said.

"Sounds great everyone. Let's meet back up in the conference room." She switched the frequency over. "Conrad, what's your position?"

"Conference room," he said.

"Great. We'll see you in a minute," she said.

She left her office and headed back down the hall and through the door to the conference room. All of the guys were standing there waiting for their orders. "We all have good communication. Everything seems to be in order and it's now ten. Conrad, who is the guy you're posting here?"

"His name is Carl Blankenship. He already has his headset on and is sitting at a computer in dispatch."

"Good, let's get the hell out of here. Grant and Ingram, radio me when you are in position. Williams, let's go," she said.

The Captain stopped them just before they made it to the elevator.

"Good luck, guys. I know we'll get him. Jordan, can I see you alone for a moment?"

She walked over to where he was standing.

"If it looks bad abort the mission. You're trained for this. These guys…well you know what I'm saying. Keep it safe out there. I'm behind you on everything, Jordan. I wouldn't have given you this case if I didn't trust you."

Jordan nodded. She knew what he was saying. Her mind was clear for the first time in weeks. All she could feel was her stomach tightening with nervousness. *Shake it off, Jordan.*

All of the cars left together and went in opposite directions. None of the team noticed Callie sitting in a parked car across the road watching them. She pulled out behind them following Jordan's car when everyone split apart.

The butterflies in the detective's stomach had turned to stone once she was on location at the bridge. She dropped Lance off at the other end and watched him walk about fifteen yards to his position. Grant and Ingram radioed that they were on location and in position. She was the last to join them after parking the car and jogging back towards the bridge.

"Conrad and Blankenship, everyone's settled. I'll get back to you guys when we get our first sighting or piece of information," she radioed.

"Yes Ma'am. My other officers and I are within two miles of each end of the bridge."

"Roger." She broke transmission and switched back to her field guys.

"Okay guys, it's getting close to eleven. Here we go. Remember, anything suspicious at all, radio me and I'll have it checked out. No one moves alone. We go on my command," she said.

Jordan was sitting in the grass and halfway tangled in a bush by the edge of the North end of the bridge. Her binoculars were set on every passing vehicle. So far, nothing looked out of the ordinary. She radioed a few tag numbers of trucks and vans that passed by, but no one stopped or slowed on the bridge. Jordan began feeling at home again. She'd spent most of her time in Washington doing undercover work. This was her specialty during her training and field of expertise as a detective. *You're on my turf now asshole, make your move.*

CHAPTER NINE

"Command to Grant and Ingram, how are things over there?" Jordan hoped someone would see something, anything to help her cut the wicked images from her head and put a stop to this guy's charade.

"Nothing yet," Grant answered quickly. Ingram following right behind him, "I haven't seen anything either. It's pretty quiet tonight."

"Williams, what about you? Anything happening on your end?"

"No, nothing except for the bushes poking my ass," he said.

"Listen, this will work. We have to give him time." *Garrison had five, then Rachel. This guy has five now. Who will be six? Damn it, who will it be? It's me he wants, it has to be, I'm supposed to be six. Garrison missed me, I was supposed to be his number six. Damn, Jordan, forget about this you have a job to do. You could be wrong. Concentrate, you have to be smarter than he is. Especially this time.*

~

A dark blue SUV drove by a few minutes later. Lance was quick on the plates, his binoculars fixed on the letter and number sequence. "Williams to Command, PQZ 768, it's a dark blue Ford Explorer."

"I see it coming my way. Let's see, there's a male driving, but I can't get a good view. His windows are too dark." She quickly changed the frequency. "Command to Conrad, I have a visual on a dark blue Explorer, plates PQZ 768. Again that's Paul, Quarter, Zebra, Seven, Six, Eight. Do you copy?" Jordan sat there waiting patiently.

"Yes, ma'am, it's running now," Blankenship said. He sat in the squeaky desk chair, staring at the minimal information that popped up immediately on the screen. "Command, that tag's clear and current on a 2008 Ford Explorer registered to Dickerson, Andrew W, out of San Francisco."

"Good, print everything out and leave it aside for me with the others. I'll collect them all when we return," she radioed back.

They waited around another twenty minutes receiving a few more male names as vehicles passed by the bridges when a dark colored car rode by heading away from Jordan and into Lance's line of sight. Jordan thought the car looked similar to Callie's, but she wasn't sure in the darkness. *She wouldn't be out here. Besides, she doesn't know we're here.*

That same blue Explorer was following a couple hundred yards or so behind it. Jordan watched as the car pulled over on the side of the bridge and the Explorer kept going.

"Williams, are you watching this?" she radioed. She was worried when she saw a woman step out of the car. The figure was closer to Lance since she parked towards his end of the bridge.

"Lieutenant, it's a woman...I think...Lieutenant, it's Dr. Marceau. Oh man, what's she doing here? I have to stop her," he radioed back.

"Lance, listen to me you can't break cover. Try to call her cell if you have your phone. I left mine on my fucking desk. We have to get her out of here. Damn it!" She was scared now. Callie was in her line of sight, but she knew something was off with the Explorer coming back by. She was at the other end of the bridge.

"I don't have my phone either," he said.

"Yell her name. Damn it," she said.

Lance called Callie's name. She didn't hear him as she kept walking towards the middle looking over the rail and down at the water. Lance was screaming her name trying to warn her to leave. He slammed his hand against his ear, yelling into the mic.

"I can't get her attention. She can't hear me! Fuck," He didn't know how to get her out of there without breaking cover.

"Okay, calm down, Lance. We have to get her out of there. I don't want to abort the mission, not yet." Jordan was trembling with fear, trying not to let on to Lance that she was scared to death.

"Grant and Ingram, we have a situation, Dr. Marceau is here. She's in the middle of the bridge alone and out of her car. I'm not aborting it just yet. She seems to be safe at the moment."

"Roger," they both radioed.

"Conrad? Do you copy?" Jordan radioed the other frequency.

"Yes, ma'am."

"We have a situation on the Golden Gate Bridge. I'm going to need your officer on the North end to make a casual pass across the bridge. The Medical Examiner working this case just stopped her car and is walking the bridge. I need the officer to get her off the bridge immediately, but casually," Jordan radioed.

"Roger. I'm actually on that end so I'll go get her myself," he radioed back.

"Sit tight, Lance. Conrad is on the way to get her," Jordan radioed on the other frequency.

"Lieutenant, here comes that Explorer and he's slowing down." Lance was almost standing. He was ready to run after the doctor.

"Damn it! Run Lance, abort mission. I repeat abort mission!" Jordan yelled into the radio and flew out of the bushes running full speed towards the other end of the bridge with her gun drawn. "Conrad, abort mission! We have a vehicle stopping next to the doctor on the bridge. Go with lights and sirens, now!"

Jordan was still running as fast as she could across the high bridge. She heard the sirens in the distance as the Explorer stopped next to Callie. A moderately built white male jumped out and grabbed her. Jordan raised her gun to fire, but she didn't want to hit Lance who was running towards them from the other end of the bridge.

The guy threw Callie kicking and screaming into his truck. The Explorer spun around in the opposite direction heading back towards Jordan and kicking up a trail of dust from the road. Jordan fired her gun emptying her automatic into the vehicle as it passed her.

"Fuck...god damn it!" she screamed. She was furious and scared.

Conrad appeared in the cruiser picking up Lance as the Explorer reached the opposite end of end of the bridge. Jordan jumped in when he got to her. Conrad took them to Jordan's car quickly and raced off trying to catch up to the speeding Explorer. Jordan and Lance took off in their unmarked car right behind Conrad's cruiser. They hit speeds in excess of a hundred mph on the interstate trying to catch the SUV. She called back into her radio. "Grant, Ingram, he's headed towards Sausalito. The son of a bitch has Dr. Marceau."

"We just turned onto the Golden Gate Bridge. We're about ten or fifteen miles behind you," Ingram radioed back while Grant drove. They had the other police cruiser behind them with the lights and siren wailing.

Jordan's haunting images returned in full color outlining Callie's face. Her stomach was tumbling over and over as she held back the urging need to vomit. She was trembling out of control. *Please God, no. Don't let him hurt her! Take me instead. I'm the one you want god damn it. Take me!*

An hour later, all of the police cars pulled over in Sonoma after they lost sight of the speeding SUV. Jordan emerged from the car she was driving and walked to the front of the group. No one could tell she was choking back the tears and frustration of watching him grab Callie before she could get to her. She stared straight ahead speaking loud and clear.

"There's an APB out on the tag and description of the vehicle. I want everyone to split up. Grant, you and Ingram continue out towards Berkley and Oakland. Williams, you'll accompany me back towards the City." She paused looking at Conrad. "Split your guys up and head towards Novato and Napa."

Jordan didn't move a muscle in her tight body as she continued talking. "Listen up, I'm positive he'll be moving back towards San Francisco. That's where he lives. The captain has a team right now watching the address on his license. I doubt it's actually his real address. This bastard is smart, but we'll get him." *I hope, before he hurts Callie. God, I can't let him hurt you, Callie.*

"Everyone meet back at the station in two hours. Remember, none of this goes through the news. If you see a reporter, turn around. If you see the vehicle, radio me with your location," Jordan said.

"I'm worried about Cal...um...Dr. Marceau.," Lance's said shakily as they got back into the unmarked car.

"I know, so am I. We'll get to her. It's not..." *Her. It's me he wants.* Her voice trailed off into her head. "We can't think the worst right now, Lance. If we do, she's gone."

~

Jordan and Lance rode around town looking up and down every street they could think of until it was close to time to head back to meet the others. They passed by the house on the address, which turned out to belong to an elderly couple with no ties to the name on the license.

Back at the station, Jordan grabbed the printed information on the driver of the SUV and went to her office. *There has to be a fucking connection. Who are you? She opened her files and the notes she wrote down when she was in D.C. This guy's name on his license and registration is Andrew W. Dickerson. You have to be Andrew Dexon, Weston Garrison's cousin. That's how you know of me, of my past.*

"Damn it, you son of a bitch!"

She searched through the rest of her files. If it was in fact Garrison's cousin, then it would all make sense. Jordan walked out of her office and over to the kitchen

135

area on the right side of the cubicles. The pot of coffee was almost empty and ice cold. "Shit!" She had been up for almost twenty four hours and was damn near running on only the adrenaline rushing through her veins. She gave up the idea of having a nasty, cold cup of old coffee and made her way down the hallway to the conference room.

"Conrad, I need to see you for a second," she said.

He followed her outside of the room and shut the door.

"I need you to run the name Andrew Weston Dexon in as many forms as you can along with as many aliases as the computer can come up with. I need all of the addresses and license photos of him. Bring it in to me as soon as you're finished."

"Yes, Ma'am." He went over to the computer desk and she walked in the other direction towards the Captain's office.

"Sir…" she said opening the door.

"Before you say anything, Jordan, it's not your fault. She didn't know what you were doing. You have a briefing to give to your team. Let's go," he said.

Jordan stood at the head of the group with her fists clinched and her knuckles down on the table, staring around at all of the men and the few women sitting in front of her. A few more officers were standing around the back of the rectangle shaped wooden table and leaning against the wall. All of the patrol officers and detectives had been called in on a 11-99 situation meaning one of their own was down and all assistance was required.

Even under severe pressure, Jordan was calm. This was serious. None of the patrol officers or even the other detectives had ever faced a situation like this. Jordan knew if she showed any sign of fear or anguish it was over. This small group of team members trusted her knowledge and her judgment, and on top of that, Callie trusted Jordan with her life.

"The search expanding through Wine Country and back to the Bay Area will continue until daylight. I have a few aliases and other addresses coming out of the system now. When it's finished, I'll have a few of you splitting up to cover those sections. The rest of us will form a search party here around town. I want everyone working in pairs..."

Conrad walked into the room with the names and addresses. There were fifteen different alias names and twenty addresses located all over town.

Jordan stepped aside with Conrad. "Did you get everything I asked for?"

"Yes, ma'am. I found most of the information on Andrew Dexon in the Washington, DC area. The pictures match though. It's the same guy. How did you know?"

"I figured that much. Let's just say it was a lucky guess." *Damn you, Andrew, don't hurt her. Callie, I'll find you. I promise I'll find you.*

Jordan walked over to the map of the city that stretched across the wall. She picked up a box of multicolored push pins. "Here are the possible hostage addresses." She put one pin on the map at each of the locations as she called them off. There were twenty of them spread out all over town. *She has to be at one of these. God, please let her be alive.*

Jordan broke the group up by location. "Grant, you and Ingram check out the Richmond, Haight Ashbury, Sunset and Twin Peaks areas. Conrad, take one of your officers with you and cover North Beach, China Town, Nob Hill, and South Beach." She looked over at the other uniformed patrol officers and detectives in the room. "The rest of you pair up and take the addresses from Filmore south through Castro, and all the way to the airport. Williams, you and I will check out Pacific Heights, Cow Hollow and Russian Hill. Everyone has access to me through your radio. I'll be in touch with Grant, Ingram, and Conrad through our mics. If you find anything or see anything, I want to be the first to know about it," she said passing around a few different pictures of Andrew as well as copies of the addresses to every pair of officers.

"Everyone has the license plate and description of the vehicle. Go through the addresses and highlight the ones that are in your assigned area. Are there any questions?" She looked around and no one made a comment."Okay, it appears we all understand what's going on here. I'll be in contact with everyone on the road. No one moves on him unless I say. We go on my orders."

Everyone left the room heading in different directions of town to search for Callie. Jordan went into the weapons locker and refilled the clip in her automatic since she'd emptied it on the truck at the bridge. The Captain followed behind her and shut the door.

"You have this well under control, Lieutenant. I'm glad to see I put the right person in command. I'll remain here with Blankenship listening for updates. I'll have the rest of the officers on Conrad's squad riding the streets and ready to go on your order."

Jordan nodded. She wasn't sure what to say any longer. Her heart was racing and her mind was flashing a kaleidoscope of pictures swirling from Callie to all of the dead bodies to Rachel and back again swirling them all together. She quickly left the room and met up with Lance who was standing outside by the car.

"Lieutenant, I'm not going to ask you how you know about this guy, even though it is my business because I'm just as much assigned to this case as you are. I am going to ask that you tell me if you think he's going to kill her. I just…I need to know. You're the only one that seems to know this asshole's every move," he said.

Jordan could hear the pain in Lance's voice. He wasn't able to hide his feelings for the beautiful doctor. Jordan couldn't help feeling the same emotions for Callie, unfortunately hers were extremely intense. She'd had the opportunity to feel those same emotions returned from Callie.

"Lance, I'm only going to say this once It's not about the identity of the kidnapped, the hostage, or the victim, it's about stopping the killer before his next move. I know you have feelings for her. I know how hard it has been for you to keep them hidden, but you can't jeopardize her life now by letting those feelings surface. Do you hear me?"

"I understand that, but…"

"Lance, listen to me, he's not going to kill her, not if I can stop him. I don't know his next move, god damn it. I don't know any of his moves. I want to find her just as much as you do and sitting here discussing this isn't going to help either of us."

~

"Denali, this is Grant, do you copy?"

"Yes, Grant, go ahead."

"We've been through two of the addresses in Richmond and Haight Ashbury and we've seen nothing. Both of the houses had new occupants. One of them said she was renting from a man that looked very similar to the pictures. She said his name was Garret Dexon."

Jordan's jaw tightened. "Has she seen her landlord lately?"

"No, there are no rent checks. It's rent cash that she puts in an envelope in a Post Office Box every month. She says she hasn't spoken with him in about four months."

"Does she have a way of contacting him?"

"She said yes, but it's through that P.O. Box. She leaves him a note and he replies back in there. If there is a problem with the house, he sends a crew of workers out to fix the problem. The only reason she ever saw his face was because she was late for a payment and he showed up at the house."

"Okay, get the address and box number from her and keep moving. I'll take care of it from here. Which address is it?"

"It's number two on the list," he said.

Jordan grabbed the list of addresses and pulled over on the right side of Sutter Street. She switched her radio frequency with the touch of a button.

"Blankenship, I need a surveillance team at address number two. He has ties to the house. It's an older single woman living there," she said.

"Yes Ma'am, I'll get right on it."

Jordan switched the radio back. "Conrad, have you seen anything?"

"No, Ma'am. No one seems to know him at any of

these addresses."

"Keep looking. He's out there somewhere. Do any of the other addresses pay their rent through a P.O. Box?"

"No," he radioed back.

~

The sun had completely risen and the time was inching closer to eight a.m. They had been searching for five hours. Jordan's body was exhausted, she was barely sleeping at night as it was, and now she'd been up over twenty four hours with her mind spinning alone through the treacherous memories of her past. They were irreversible, no matter how hard she tried to make it stop, Callie's body took the place of Rachel's in the graphic images of her lying on the floor in a pool of blood. *Oh god, Callie, I'm so sorry. I should have protected you. I let him get you. I'll find you, if it takes all day and night. I'm not going to let him hurt you. Not you!*

Jordan pulled over at a small coffee house outside of the neighborhood. She got out of the car, speaking under her breath. "Damn it, Jordan, you have to get yourself together." *You can't do this, not here, not now. Callie needs you.*

"Ah, …hi, I would like a large decaf, white chocolate mocha and two slices of pound cake. Lance?" She looked over at him staring into the air with a lost blank look on his face. "Lance!" She had to raise her voice to get his attention.

"Sorry, I was thinking about something else. I'll have a large um…a large mint mocha and two chocolate chip muffins, thanks. Hey, why did you order unleaded coffee? Are you a damn robot or something? I'm so tired

141

I can't see straight."

Jordan looked at him while contemplating telling him to kiss her ass. "I can't have the caffeine, it's a long story. Besides, you should worry about yourself. You look like shit."

When their order was ready they went back to the car trying not to notice the abundance of stares coming from the people behind the counter as well as the other customers in the room. Jordan and Lance had both long forgotten about the G.I. Joe outfits they were wearing.

They sat in the car eating breakfast and drinking coffee while trying to keep their eyelids from closing. Even if they wanted to, neither of them could sleep at this point. Lance was directly participating in a career making case and Jordan was wrapped up in another dramatic event with a mastermind serial killer taking her head on. *Why the hell does this shit always happen to me? I swear karma is a bitch.*

Just as they were beginning to pull away Grant came across the radio yelling.

"Lieutenant! I have a visual on the Explorer. The plates have been changed, but I'm sure it's the truck. It has bullet holes along the front and the side."

"Okay, calm down Grant where are you?"

"Umm…hell where the fuck are we? Oh, okay we just turned off of Market onto Filmore Street."

"You're not in pursuit are you?" she asked.

"No, well, yes, but we're at a safe distance."

"Okay, stay way back at least five or six cars. If he knows you're tailing him then he'll take off. I'm about two blocks away coming head on with you."

Jordan sped through the traffic and cut over onto a side road and came back out in front of Grant. "Captain,

142

we have a visual on the SUV. He's moving North on Filmore. I'm in a distant pursuit with Grant behind me. Don't send anyone close. Keep the backup cars at least two blocks over parallel to me. If he sees them he'll run," she radioed.

"Roger that, I have two cars in your immediate area and another a few blocks away."

The radio went silent as they followed the dark blue Explorer into the Pacific Heights district full of old Victorian homes. Finally, it began to slow down. *I got your ass now you son of a bitch!*

"Grant, he's stopping at that house up there, turn off to the left here behind me," Jordan radioed.

She jumped out of the car with Lance right behind her. Grant parked along the curb behind her.

"Blankenship, run this plate, QDS 141."

"Yes, ma'am, wait a minute. The plate is coming up registered to a woman Yader, Susan on a 1997 Oldsmobile, white."

Jordan was mildly confused. *Maybe this woman knew Andrew as one of his aliases and he changed the tag without her knowledge. Who knows.*

"Okay guys, we don't have a positive ID on the SUV or the tag. There could be another woman in the house also. We need to approach quietly on foot. I want you to go to the front door with two patrol officers, Ingram. Ask for his cooperation and permission to look around. The rest of you patrol officers split up and cover the windows on the sides of the house. Grant, you and Williams will come around the back and enter with me. If he answers the door and we have a positive ID radio me. I'll order the go ahead. Everyone got it?"

CHAPTER TEN

Lance and Grant were beside Jordan as they squatted behind the back door. She heard a loud noise and Ingram was screaming on the radio.

"We have a positive ID! He took off running towards the back of the house. We're inside, but we've lost him!"

Jordan busted through the back door, her forty-five automatic drawn and ready to fire with Grant and Williams following her. She began yelling into her ear piece and across the house. "Split up! Everyone split up. Now!" She cleared each room quickly moving through the living area and into the kitchen on the first floor. There was no sign of him or Callie.

"Captain, we're inside. He's in here somewhere. Ingram lost him when he came to the front door."

"Copy that. Be careful, Jordan. The back up team should be there within two minutes."

Jordan searched the first floor until she found the basement door. She called for Williams and Grant to back her up. Everyone else was spread throughout the house. The door was apparently dead bolted shut from the inside and none of them could kick it in.

"God damn it!" Jordan backed up with the two guys and each fired a shot into the door jam. Jordan lunged forward with all of her weight kicking the bulleted area and the door cracked along the bolted locks. Grant and Williams followed her action, kicking with all of their weight at the door until it was finally broken open.

~

Jordan moved slowly into the darkness and down the stairs turning towards the back of the house when she reached the bottom. Grant and Williams went in different directions searching the separated rooms with their flashlights. The basement was sectioned off with four small bedrooms like an additional floor of the house. *Callie! I'll find you. I have to find you!* She checked briefly in one room before heading towards the end of hall.

Jordan went up to the last door on the right side of the narrow hallway. The knob was locked so she reared back and kicked right above the handle. The knob broke and she went flying out of the dark hallway and into the dimly lit room. She could barely make out the figures in front of her.

"Let her go, Andrew! Damn you, let her go now!" Jordan found him standing next to Callie who was unconscious and laying in the semi-darkness on a metal table with what looked like an IV needle stuck into her arm. Williams and Grant heard Jordan yelling and quickly ran towards the sound. They managed to find each other in the darkness, their flashlights scanning the area that they thought Jordan was in.

"Where is she, Grant?"

"God damn it, I don't know. It sounded like it was coming from over here," Grant said. They both went to the left looking high and low for an entrance to the small room Jordan was in.

"I see you've made it just in time, Denali. I've saved

you a front row seat," Andrew sneered.

He was standing there with a syringe stuck in the IV dangling from Callie's right arm. Jordan couldn't see what he was about to give her or had already given her. The room was too dark and she was holding her automatic with both hands. She'd dropped her flashlight when she kicked in the door.

"If you come any closer, Denali, I'll have to let her go faster than I want to. You should drop that gun too. It's only going to make this worse. You can't save her. You're too late, just like you were four years ago. You don't seem to have it anymore. You get too caught up in your women to pay attention to your job. I thought Weston showed you that."

Jordan stepped forward and set her automatic on the concrete floor in front of her feet. The room was almost completely black except for a small light over by the table that Callie was laying on.

"Andrew, put the needle down. Don't hurt her. She has nothing to do with this. It's me you want."

"Oh but you see, Detective, you're wrong. I want you to be in my shoes and watch someone close to you die of these lethal poisons while you can't stop it. See, you let them take Weston from me and I had to watch in silence as he died on that cold metal table like a lab rat. Now, I'm going to take her from you. Someone has to teach you a lesson," he said pushing the back of the syringe. The injection began flowing through the lines.

Just as Jordan reached down to her left pant leg for the 9mm Andrew came around the side on the table and lunged towards her knocking her forward to the ground. She was able to find her automatic on the cold cement in front of her and fired off a shot into the darkness at the shadow she could barely see facing her. The figure fell rapidly to the ground. Jordan jumped up from the floor and snatched the IV out of Callie's arm picking her up off of the table. She struggled to get the door open while cradling Callie's limp body against her. *Hold on, Callie, please just hold on. It'll be over soon, I promise.*

Williams and Grant heard the shot and raced towards the door. They were barely able to make out Jordan's shape as she came out carrying Callie.

"He's in there. I think I got him, but it was dark. I couldn't see. Move!" she yelled.

"Is she..."

"Lance, go with Grant, god damn it!"

"Conrad, radio your guys. I'm coming out with Callie. She's unconscious," Jordan radioed.

"Yes, Ma'am. I have an ambulance waiting around the corner. Is it safe?"

"No, the house is not secure. I repeat no, we are not secure! I got a shot off, but I don't know if I hit him. It was too dark to see anything," she said.

Jordan appeared, seconds later, walking out of the front door still carrying Callie in her arms. The adrenaline was flowing through her veins so fiercely her body didn't feel the strain of carrying a person her own size. She didn't notice the thick stream of blood running down the right side of her own face either.

Jordan met up with the ambulance parked a few houses down. The EMT's had the stretcher out and were wheeling it towards her.

"He had an IV in her arm and also shot her up with something in a syringe. I think it may have been the stuff they use for lethal injections," she said placing Callie's cold, limp body onto the stretcher. She jumped in the back with the attending EMT and the other one shut the doors before driving off with the siren screeching and the lights flashing.

"Ingram, Grant, do you have a copy?" Jordan radioed on the way to the hospital.

"Lieutenant, this is Lance, you got him. Do you hear me? You got his ass!"

"What was that? Come back, Williams! Is he dead?"

"Yes, Ma'am, that's affirmative. You shot him between the eyes. He has no pulse and a huge ass hole in the back of his head."

Oh thank God. Please, Callie, you have to be okay.

~

Lance took charge and cleared the scene. After all of the other police officers were gone he made his statement to the press, and then he left the paperwork details to Grant and Ingram before heading to the hospital to check on Callie. Since Jordan wasn't answering her radio he wasn't sure if she was hurt or not. It was too dark to see either of them when she came out of the room carrying Callie.

"Captain, have you heard anything?" Lance radioed.

"No, I'm not sure what's going on. The Doctor and Lieutenant Denali are both at San Francisco General Hospital. That's all I know. How are things out there Lance? Is everything cleared up?"

"Yes, Sir. The M.E. van just left with the body and the press has their statement. If you don't mind…"

"No, go ahead, I know you want to go to the hospital to check on Jordan. I'm sure she's fine. Tell Ingram and Grant to take charge of the scene."

"Thanks Sir, I'll update you when I get there."

~

"Damn you, leave me alone. I'm fine! She's the one you should be looking at, not me."

"Officer, please. You have a bad cut on your head. We need to check it out," one of the doctors said to Jordan.

"Damn it, if you touch me one more time so help me I'm going to choke you with that stethoscope that's around your neck!"

Jordan wouldn't leave the trauma room that Callie was in. She stood back watching the doctors run around frantically giving Callie shots and IV fluids to counteract against the poisons that Andrew gave her. *She has to be okay. Please don't take her from me. I can't lose her too!*

All of the medication had caused a reaction in Callie's nervous system sending her into a coma. The doctor had placed an endotrachal tube and hooked it up to a ventilator to help control her breathing and decided the only thing left to do was wait it out and see if she woke up.

"Please, let me have a few minutes with her. Then you can do whatever you want to my fucking head," Jordan sneered.

The doctor backed away and left her alone at Callie's bedside in the Trauma Unit. Jordan sat there holding Callie's right hand in hers as small tears began slowing flowing down her face.

"I'm sorry, Callie. I'm so sorry. I didn't...I should have moved in quicker to get you away from him. I failed you. I didn't protect you and for that I am truly sorry.

Please wake up, you have to wake up. Callie, please. I don't think I can handle you leaving me too."

Jordan finally realized the aching in her head was causing some blurriness in Callie's face as she looked down at her. She sat the soft cold hand back on the bed. They had been in the hospital for over two hours and something was definitely wrong. She stood up and walked towards the door to find the nurse, but she was too dizzy to make out the people standing in front of her as she collapsed.

~

Lance was pointed in the direction of the trauma rooms when he arrived at the hospital. He saw Jordan at Callie's beside through the window. She was sitting with her back to him. He turned towards Harvey McCormick, who was standing on the other side of the hallway next to the nurse's station.

"I'm sure Jordan will want something to eat or drink when she comes out of there. I'm going down to the cafeteria. Do you need anything?"

"No thanks, I'll be fine," Harvey said staring at the closed door to Callie's room.

Lance returned from the cafeteria with a small cup of coffee and a banana. He noticed Jordan was gone from Callie's room and a doctor was in there with her.

"Is everything okay? Did she wake up?" he asked.

"No, she hasn't woken up yet. Detective Denali has a serious cut on her forehead and a concussion. She got dizzy and fell right after you left, but she's ok. They took her for a CT Scan and probably a few stitches," he said looking down at Lance's hand. "Is that a banana? There must not be much to chose from down there."

"Yeah, nothing looked appealing to me." He laughed slightly thinking about Jordan's reaction to him bringing her a banana and stale coffee. He remembered he needed to call the captain so he stepped to the opposite side of the hallway dialing the number.

"Captain, it's Lance."

"Are you at the hospital?" the Captain asked.

"Yes. Dr. Marceau is in a coma. The doctor says she'll probably wake up and be fine, but there is a chance she might not wake up at all or have neurological complications. It depends on how far the lethal injection fluid traveled through her circulatory system."

"Oh my god, I hope she's going to be okay. Is there any word on Jordan? Have you seen her? I haven't spoken to her yet."

"She was in Callie's room when I arrived. I haven't talked to her, but I heard she has a bad cut on her head and may have a concussion or head injury that caused her to collapse in Callie's room. They took her to get her head checked out and get cleaned up. She'll probably need some stitches. I'm not sure if you know this or not, but Jordan dropped him with one shot in the dark. I don't kn…"

"Yes Lance, I know she might be a pain in the ass around here, but the woman is good, damn good! I would trust her with my own life if I had to."

~

A few hours later, Jordan was stitched up and fighting to be released. She had a concussion that would require rest and in her opinion there was no significant injury to her head. She finally signed out Against Medical Advice and walked over to the nurse's station to use the phone.

"Captain, it's Jordan."

"How are you? Lance said you were hurt? Is everything okay?" he asked.

"Yes, Sir. I'm fine. I have eight stitches above my right eye, but no…"

"Jesus, Jordan, you shouldn't be up moving around," he screeched.

"Sir, I'm fine, really, I don't have any fractures or anything. The doctor said it's just a concussion at the most. I must have hit my head on the metal table when he jumped on me."

"Damn, you went through hell, Jordan. I'll expect a full report when you return to work next week."

"Next week? Excuse me?"

"You're on medical leave until next week. I don't want to hear any buts about it. Besides, this case is over and your pending suspension starts after you turn in your paperwork. You need some time off to get your head better and sort through this mess. I don't want to see you back here for a week. I mean it, Lieutenant Denali. That is a direct order."

"Yes, Sir. I'll return next week as you wish. I need to…I should probably,"

"Go check on the doctor and find Lance. He's around there somewhere. Make him go home. You guys have all been up for God knows how long," he said.

"Yes, Sir," she said hanging up.

Damn it, I was hoping he forgot about the whole suspension thing. I can't worry about that right now. I have to see Callie. I'm sure I can find Lance hovering around her room.

~

Jordan walked towards the trauma unit. She stopped a nurse to ask where they had put Callie. Her head was still throbbing with pain and she had forgotten what room Callie was in. The nurses gave her directions and she proceeded down the hallway to the right. Lance was standing against the glass staring into Callie's room through the window. Harvey McCormick was across from him leaning along the wall.

"Lieutenant, how are you feeling?" Harvey asked.

"I'm fine. Thank you, Doctor," she said.

"Damn, it looks like you took a beating yourself there, Super Woman." Lance tried to lighten the subject slightly. He knew Jordan had to be in pain from the looks of the nasty stitches above her bruised and swollen black eye.

"I'm no Super Woman, Williams, only an average, everyday Homicide Detective. I just happened to walk into the right room and take a lucky shot."

"Bullshit, I was there. I saw his body. You dropped his ass with that one shot and in the dark no less. Come on, Lieutenant, give yourself some credit here. You're lucky to be alive. He could have seriously hurt you."

"It's over, Williams. I've spoken to the captain and he said to tell you it's time for you to call it a day, or night, or whatever and go home. He also advised me to turn in my paperwork on this case and take a week off to heal my head," she said.

"I really think someone should..."

"Lance, that is a direct order. Go home. I'm sure Dr.

153

McCormick will stay here with Dr. Marceau."

Lance nodded his head looking into Callie's room one last time. He walked down the hallway as Jordan walked into Callie's room. She stood next to her bed gently picking up her right hand as she spoke.

"Callie, I'm sorry you're lying here. It should be me. Damn it. It should be me. You have to wake up. I can't bend down and kiss your cheek with the window blinds open. I...God, please wake up, Callie. I need you." The tears were too strong to hold back as Jordan placed Callie's hand back onto the bed next to her still body. She cleared her throat and wiped her eyes before leaving the room. The attending doctor walked in as she was leaving.

"Is she...um...can you tell me if sh..."

"She's going to be fine. I'm sure she'll wake up sometime tonight with the worst headache she's ever felt and be eager to get out of here. The medication is straining her system right now causing her body to be extremely weak. Once she has rested she'll regain consciousness. All of her vital signs are excellent," he said.

"Thank you. Thank you for everything," Jordan said walking away.

"It's you who should be thanked. You're the one who saved her."

I didn't save her. I'm the reason she's lying in there. Damn it don't you people see, it's my fault.

Jordan walked out into the hallway and over to Dr. McCormick. He was still leaning against the wall peering into the window at the doctor checking on Callie.

"Here's my card. Can you please..."

"Lieutenant, I'm not sure what happened out there. I'm not sure I really want to know, but what I do know, is everyone is calling you a hero around here," he said.

"I'm no hero. It's my fault she's in there," Jordan said firmly fighting back the tears that were filling in her dark blue eyes.

"I'll call you as soon as she wakes up and if I hear any more news you'll be the first to know," he said.

"Thank you."

~

Jordan walked into her penthouse suite, placing her Kevlar vest on the table as she crossed the living room area. Standing next to her bed, she stripped out of the fatigue uniform and combat boots. Naked, she slipped into her short, gray, silk robe. She stopped in front of the long mirror on the wall next to the closet door. She reached her right hand up to her face gracing her fingers across the threads above her right eye. The stitches were just as swollen and bruised as her eye was.

"Damn, I look like shit! Ouch!"

She hated leaving Callie at the hospital, but she hadn't slept in nearly thirty six hours. It would be almost impossible to try and sleep knowing Callie was still not out of the woods completely. *You really fucked up this time Jordan. How could you not check him out when you knew it was all over? This is what you're trained for and you let him slip right by you.* She couldn't stop the thoughts from ripping through her head.

The moonlight glistened through the large floor to ceiling bay windows in the living area. Jordan stood against the bar sipping a neat glass of scotch. As a result of not being able to chase the ghosts from her mind, she decided to drown them out. She finally dozed off curled up on the couch.

Her cell phone rang loudly at three a.m. "Damn it, where the fuck is my phone?" Jordan searched for the loud ringing noise half asleep and half out of her mind from the uncontrollable throbbing pain in her head.

"Denali...Hello...Hello?"

"Detective, it's Harvey."

"Sorry...is she awake?"

"She woke up about ten minutes ago, although she's very groggy from the medication. She's asking for you," he said.

Jordan stood there in awe for a second that felt like a minute. *She probably wants to tear my head off. She...I can't go up there. I can't go see her, not like this. Oh Callie, I want to be with you too, so bad it's killing me, but you can never know how I feel about you. I'll only continue to hurt you if I let you in.*

"Uh Detective? Are you still there? Hello?"

"Yeah, sorry, uh tell her I'll see her in the morning. I have to go back for a check-up myself and I'll stop in to see her then. Thanks for calling," she said.

"Sure. Goodnight, Detective."

~

The alarm clock rang out as usual at five a.m., Jordan sat up untangling the black, silk bed sheets that were wrapped around her naked body. She only slept for a few hours, dozing in and out of terrible nightmares. The actions of the past few days left her body in a state of extreme exhaustion, yet she still managed to crawl out of bed and force herself to take a shower. Going to the gym was out of the question with the concussion.

The hot shower was the closest thing to a massage that she could think of. As soon as she was dried off, she dressed in a pair of black casual slacks, a baby blue polo shirt, and black leather shoes. Even in casual attire she dressed to impress wearing only designer clothing.

She grabbed her wallet with her badge and locked her gun and its holster in the wall safe next to the ammo cartridges and tucked her smaller, backup pistol into the holster at the back of her pants since she was officially on medical leave. She didn't trust herself to shoot anything with her head pounding as bad as it was, but she didn't want to be unprotected on the streets. Outside of the building she waved down a taxi since she wasn't up to riding the trolley. She refused to take any medication for it and the pain was starting to make her agitated.

The hospital was busy when she first arrived. Thankfully, the nurse called her name only minutes after she sat down in the waiting room.

"Please follow me," the nurse said. "Dr. Fitzgerald is expecting you."

The young nurse took the detective directly towards Callie's room. Jordan wasn't sure why since she was there to have a check up on her head injury. Hospitals weren't her favorite place and she didn't show her face in one unless she was dying or someone close to her was.

"Lieutenant, how are you feeling this morning?" The doctor met up with her right outside of Callie's closed door.

Hmm, let's see...like shit! How do you think I feel? Smart ass! My head's about to fucking explode! "I'm not too bad. My head is still sore. I'll live, right?" Jordan's mouth raised up in one corner. The doctor smiled back at her.

"Yes, you're going to be fine, if you let that head of yours rest. I'll give you a different prescription for the pain and you'll be on your way You should be back to your old self in a few days. The stitches will need to come out in about seven days." He reached up and put a small amount of pressure around the threads above Jordan's right eye.

"Ouch!" Jordan jerked back away from him.

"Sorry about that. It looks like it's going to heal up just fine. You probably won't need plastic surgery or anything for the scar.

Excuse me? Do I look like I...oh never mind this isn't worth my time. I've been a lot worse than this and didn't even bother coming back for a recheck. If it wasn't for Callie being in here I wouldn't be anywhere near this place right now, you idiot. "Well, that's good to know then. Thanks, Doc. By the way, I don't need the script. I never had the other one filled." Jordan stepped back to walk towards the exit doors.

"Detective Denali, this is really none of my business, but Dr. Marceau has been asking about you an awful lot. I think your partner spoke with her a little while ago. Also, I think you're a fool not to take the medication when you're obviously in pain, but suit yourself. I can't force you." He smiled at her and walked away shaking his head.

CHAPTER ELEVEN

Jordan walked up to the closed door clinching her fists tightly by her side before opening it. Callie was lying there asleep and still hooked up to a few different machines and IV lines. Jordan slowly walked over and sat in the chair next to the bed watching Callie's chest rise up and fall back down with every breath. She looked so peaceful. Jordan didn't want to wake her, but she had to touch her. She picked up Callie's warm, right hand holding it between her own two hands. Callie's body shifted slightly and her beautiful emerald green eyes opened wide when she saw Jordan holding her hand.

"Hello there stranger," Callie whispered.

"Hi yourself."

Jordan was nervous. Being in hospitals wasn't a pleasant experience to start with and her heart was racing with the desire to hold Callie. They had already shared one intimate moment, it would be too dangerous to take it any further. Jordan knew that. What she didn't know was how to fight off the feelings that were soaring out of control where this woman was concerned. Jordan didn't want to hurt Callie, but being there at her bedside was breaking every rule she swore by. *Damn it, why am I here? I shouldn't be here. I shouldn't be doing this.*

"I see your partner was right," Callie said staring at the unpleasant sight of the stitches and bruising above the detective's right eye.

Jordan noticed the beautiful eyes focused on her face. She reached one hand up to her eye but didn't make contact with her skin.

"Oh you mean this? It's nothing, I'm fine." She lied through her teeth. Showing her pain was not something she wanted to do, or even knew how to do. She was taught early in life that Marines don't know pain and later she learned that cops never show pain.

"Look at you, Jordan. You look like shit. I bet you probably haven't slept in a week. Your face is cut and bruised. You went through hell too and you act like your life is nothing. I hate to see you like this. You don't have to be so god damn strong all the time. You're human, Jordan, just like everyone else in this world."

Jordan was still holding Callie's hand, trying desperately not to upset her. "Callie, listen to me please. I don't know what Lance told you, but..."

"He told me you found me. You saved my life, Jordan."

"Well, it's not that easy. I'm no hero. I was only doing my job. It's my fault..."

"What's your fault? I don't understand, Jordan. Don't blame yourself. You had no way of knowing this would happen." Callie could see Jordan's sapphire eyes glimmering with the bright lights on the ceiling.

"Do you remember anything that occurred before or after I found you?" Jordan asked.

"No, only what I've been told, which isn't much. Lance said that you found me and rode with me to the hospital."

"Yes, that's correct. I didn't know I was hurt until I arrived here. The medics were trying to help you. I don't even remember them looking at me. If they tried I probably refused." Jordan believed it was best for Callie not to know everything that happened in that dark room.

"I bet you did, Detective. You seem to have everything under control well over a hundred percent of the time. You always put yourself last."

"It's my job, Callie, twenty four hours a day, seven days a week, fifty two weeks a year. I'm a Homicide Detective. It's my job to put the victims first, always." Jordan tried not to be forceful. She didn't want to be there, not like that, not as Lieutenant Denali. She only wanted to be there as Jordan, the woman with the uncompromising feelings for Callie, but that kind of personal relationship with a colleague was forbidden and unjust in Jordan's private code of ethics within herself, as well as against everything she was sworn into.

"One day, Jordan, you will realize you have a job and you also have a life. Look, I'm not going to argue with you. I want to thank you for stopping by. Seeing you always makes me feel better." Callie's lips turned up gradually in the corners, forming a tiny smile.

"You're welcome, Callie. I was back for my follow up and I wanted to make sure you were okay. I need to get going though, duty calls and I have a ton of paperwork to take care of." Jordan said her goodbye and smiled one last time as she squeezed Callie's hand.

~

Two days had gone by since Jordan saw Callie in the hospital. She was concentrating on finishing up her paperwork and trying not to think of the only thing on her mind, Callie's beautiful green eyes and her sexy smile. Even on a medical leave of absence she continued her days as usual, waking early to go to the gym.

She had finally started making a dent in the pile of paperwork on her dining room table next to her laptop and was reminded of the fact that even on casual suspension she couldn't put her job on hold. She began wondering if workaholic was actually something you could really become, instead of an overused excuse.

Jordan was sitting at the rectangle shaped, glass table, peering out of the large living room windows into the darkness surrounding the city lights when she heard a quiet, gentle knock on the door. Jordan jumped up immediately running into the bedroom. She returned to the foyer with her loaded automatic in her hand and held it by her side. *Who the hell would be coming here tonight? No one knows where I live. The front desk didn't call and the doorman didn't ring.*

She looked through the tiny peep hole. Callie stood there staring at the wall separating them. Jordan quickly withdrew her gun and opened the door. Callie saw the question in Jordan's deep blue eyes as she stood in the doorway of the foyer.

"We need to talk, Jordan," Callie said.

"Can I get you anything?" Jordan was nervous. She wasn't necessarily shy, but agitated that Callie would barge in uninvited. She had never had anyone one else in her suite except for the housekeeper of course. Her life was private and she intended on keeping it so.

"Sure, whatever you're drinking." Callie moved over to the gray leather sofa and sat down facing the San Francisco skyline.

Jordan poured Callie a matching glass of scotch from the decanter on the bar and walked over handing it to her.

"Here you go. I...how...why are you here, Callie?"

"Whoa, what the hell is this?" Callie grimaced trying to swallow the strong drink before she spit it all over the room.

"It's scotch," Jordan said with a crooked smile on her face. "Would you like something else? I really only drink this stuff at home so I'm not sure if I have anything else here, maybe a bottle of wine, or a beer."

"No, no, this is fine. I've just never had it. This isn't the reason I'm here."

"Yes, I'm sure it isn't. Now, if you wouldn't mind filling me in on how and why you are sitting in my living room that would be greatly appreciated." Jordan sat on the loveseat adjacent to the full sofa Callie was sitting on. She was trying not be blunt, but she was feeling somewhat disturbed by Callie showing up at her door.

"As I said, we need to talk. I want the truth, Jordan. Harvey told me you fought with the doctors to stay at my bedside until you collapsed. He said you were too stubborn to have yourself checked out."

"That's somewhat true. I wasn't unconscious or anything. I sort of fainted, I guess."

"You're as stubborn as an old mule," Callie said. "I also know you not only carried me out of the house and down the road to the ambulance with your head bleeding everywhere, but you killed the guy."

"Yes, he's dead. He'll never hurt anyone again," Jordan sighed.

"Dr. Fitzgerald kept telling me he wasn't authorized to say anything about the events that took place. After I threatened to quit earlier this evening, Harvey finally told me the details about what happened. When were you planning on telling me all of this?"

"Well, I..."

"Wait, there's more. Lance said you were both there when I was taken. I can't remember anything about that day or night. He said you tried so hard to get to me. Who was he, Jordan? Damn it, I know you knew him. I know this has to do with your trip to DC. I want you to tell me about Rachel. Tell me why you were there. Why you broke down like you did? Don't shut me out, Jordan, not anymore."

"Callie, it's too complicated. This is too much, you being here. I've already gone too far and I'm sorry. Please let it go. Forget what you saw, forget what you heard. I'm sorry you were put in the middle of it. I'm so very sorry for hurting you."

Callie stood up and moved over to Jordan. She sat down taking the detective's right hand into hers. She could see the pain shadowing her eyes as they grew darker.

"I can't just let it go, Jordan. I care about you, please talk to me. I need to understand."

Jordan reached with her left hand and brushed the hair from Callie's face. Her body was trembling, yearning for this woman's touch. Callie let go of Jordan's hand and grabbed her shirt, pulling Jordan up against her as their lips met. Their tongues danced while their bodies removed the tension built by the wall between them.

Callie's hands were tangled in Jordan's hair tugging softly as Jordan ran her hands up Callie's sides under her shirt, stopping at her breasts to caress the taut nipples. Callie moved her mouth along Jordan's jaw line and up to her ear as she bit down tenderly teasing the lobe of skin between her teeth.

"Where's your bed? Jordan, take me into your bed and make love to me, please. I want to feel your naked body against me," Callie growled in a low voice.

Jordan stood quickly, pulling Callie to her feet. Wrapping her arms around Callie's waist she walked her backwards through the bedroom doorway. Next to the bed Jordan removed Callie's shirt to reveal her uncovered breasts. Callie unhooked Jordan's bra through her shirt and pulled them both over her head.

Jordan pressed her mouth to Callie's kissing her passionately as she unbuttoned Callie's jeans slipping her hand down inside. She caressed the folds between the firm legs easing her fingers through the warm moisture.

"Please Jordan, I'm so close...don't tease," Callie hissed. She could barely catch her breath as her hips thrust harder into the hand between her thighs.

"Wait, wait! I want to taste you first." Jordan snatched Callie's pants down tossing them across the room along with her thong panties. She picked Callie up laying her down on the bed as she slid her half naked body between Callie's damp legs. Her mouth stopped just below Callie's navel. Jordan lightly kissed her way down along each thigh and then back across the burning fire in the center of Callie's legs.

"God, stop teasing! Take me, Jordan, Please, I want..." Before she could finish her sentence Jordan's tongue passed over her clit, swirling in circles.

Callie let out a deep moan as she tugged softly on Jordan's hair. Jordan could feel the pressure between her own legs rising as Callie's hips thrashed against her face. She'd wanted Callie since the first day she laid eyes on her. Now, the dream she often had was coming true.

"Oh, God..." Callie said in a raspy voice as her body began to release the tension built up over the past few months.

Callie was still in Jordan's mouth, whimpering quietly from the rush of pleasure that had just passed. Jordan eased away kissing every inch of Callie's firm curves from her waist, across her breasts, and up to her neck. Their lips met once again, this time softer yet just as stimulating as before. Callie drew away slightly tasting herself for the first time. She ran her tongue along Jordan's mouth before sliding her lips against Jordan's soft cheek. Finding her ear she whispered eagerly, "I believe it is my turn, Lieutenant."

Jordan rolled onto her back pulling Callie on top of her. "And what might you have in my mind, Doctor?" Jordan growled, teasing back.

"Trust me, I promise to go easy on you." Callie winked her eye rolling her hips against Jordan's. She smiled before sliding down between the detective's legs. She ran her hands along the tightly sculpted body under her. She had never felt a body so hard, yet so very soft, sexy, and feminine.

Jordan trembled as Callie lips brushed against the tense, pulsating, mound of flesh between her thighs. It had been four long, cold years since she had made love to or with another woman. She moaned when Callie spread the folds apart with her tongue and backed away just enough to separate her mouth from Jordan's body.

"Oh God! Callie, please don't stop!" Jordan was flinching out of control. Callie forcefully put her mouth back down with the full length of her tongue gliding along the slick center dipping inside. Jordan tore at the bed sheets as Callie took her wildly over the edge ending with soft, sweet kisses on her thighs.

"Come here," Jordan whispered. She had a crooked smile on her face and her sapphire blue eyes were

166

glowing brighter than Callie had ever seen them.

Callie pressed her lips to Jordan's, their tongues slowly tangled in the slow dance of a passionate kiss. Jordan moved so that Callie's head was on the curve of her shoulder. They fell asleep wrapped in the silk sheets holding one another.

~

Jordan sat straight up in the bed with tears streaming down her face. She was screaming at the top of her lungs, "Please don't take her! No! God please don't do this to me!"

Callie awoke frightened by the screaming. She wrapped her arms around Jordan pulling her close. "Hey, it's okay. Jordan, calm down. I'm here." Callie rocked back and forth trying to calm the crying woman. She had seen her break down once before and hoped it was the first and last time she witnessed this terrifying dark pain inside of Jordan. "It's Callie, Jordan. I'm here. I promise I won't let anything hurt you. It's okay."

Jordan finally calmed down a few minutes later. Realizing where she was, she moved away from Callie wiping the tears from her face. *Not again. Not in front her. God, not like this.* Jordan turned back towards Callie, "I'm sorry."

"You don't have anything to be sorry about, Jordan. No, I don't understand, but I hope you will try to explain it to me one day." Callie leaned forward and pressed a soft kiss upon Jordan's lips. Jordan grabbed Callie's hands.

"I…" Jordan let out a long sigh. "It's been so long, Callie, I…"

"Jordan, you don't have to tell me now, it's okay." Callie squeezed Jordan's hand.

"Callie, if I don't do it now I may never attempt this again. I need to tell you. Please..." A small tear ran down her right cheek. "Please don't hate me."

"Oh Jordan, I could never hate you, everything is okay. I'm here for you now. I promise I won't go anywhere."

Jordan took a long, deep breath and slowly let it back out fighting off the tears surrounding her ocean blue eyes. *It's time, Jordan, time to let her go.*

"I went through the academy in Washington DC. Due to my military training, I was assigned to the homicide division six months later. I worked my way up the ranks through most of the smaller cases. Close to five years later, I was assigned as the lead detective on a serial homicide case. I had spoken with one of the young rookie Patrol Officers, Rachel Doyle, about a few of my other cases. She was so young, yet more intelligent than most of the other detectives. She wanted to be a detective in the Homicide Division and was completely intrigued by me. I sort of took her under my wing and began showing her the ropes." The tears began to roll over Jordan's eye lids sliding down her cheeks.

"By allowing her to view my confidential files, I broke every rule that I was sworn to. I couldn't stop it. We became so close and I let her not only into my high profile case, but also into my heart. I had never been close to anyone before I met her and against everything we were taught, we formed a relationship outside of the department. We fell so deeply in love with each other and were completely inseparable." There was a touch of happiness in Jordan's voice when she spoke of the time she shared with Rachel that made it seem like it wasn't so long ago.

"I finally figured out who the serial killer was close to a year into my relationship with Rachel. He was a thirty-eight year old mail clerk named Weston Garrison. I let my guard down being totally wrapped up in her. He was able to get closer to me. He knew I was onto him, and he taunted me for months watching my every move, going back and forth like it was a sick game of cat and mouse. I finally tracked him to a secluded location, which later turned out to be a set up for me. I sent a few patrol officers and one of the other detectives to check out another place I thought he may have been hiding.

"I headed to the secluded location with no back up, relying on pure instinct. Rachel demanded that she go with me. I couldn't stop her. I tried so hard to make her stay behind. If I had gone without her I knew she would've showed up anyway. She was just as stubborn as me.

"We arrived at the old abandoned office building and I left Rachel alone on the ground floor while I searched the second floor. I heard an ear piercing scream come from Rachel." Jordan choked back more tears as her mind remembered the awful events of that morning.

"I ran back down the stairs and she was on her knees in front of him. He waited until I was close enough to witness everything as he yelled for me to toss my gun to the floor. I put my gun down hoping he would leave her alone. He walked closer, kicking my gun away and turned back towards her with his gun raised. He shot her in the head right in front of me. I ran to her, grabbing her limp body up into my arms. He stood there shaking his head and laughing at the site of my pain just before he fled the scene."

Jordan's voice was cracking, her face was red and soaked with tears, and her eyes were as black as the night sky. Callie pulled Jordan into her arms.

"I...I held her in my arms until I felt her body let go. I called for backup, but they arrived too late to see him leaving. Callie, I left her alone. I gave her right to him. It's my fault she's gone. He wanted me and I let him take her instead." Jordan was crying so hard her entire body was trembling.

"Jordan, it wasn't your fault. You didn't know what was going to happen. I'm sure Rachel knew you loved her. She knew you didn't leave her deliberately." Callie held Jordan tight in her arms.

"I can still hear her screaming and see him standing over her bloody body laughing at me. I can't make it go away, damn it. I try so hard," Jordan said.

"I'm here for you, Jordan. I'm not going anywhere, I promise."

Jordan leaned back letting a small space form between them. "There's more, Callie. I stayed with her until her body was taken away and then I left. I walked away from everything and came here. I wasn't there for her at all. I didn't even go to the funeral. I never said goodbye to her. I ran as far away as I could. Callie, I was literally on a plane the next morning. I couldn't take it. I was tumbling down a black hole with no way out.

"Two weeks later, I finally called my captain in DC to tell him where I was and he gave me a recommendation to the captain here. I never received the suspension or termination I had coming to me for insubordination because of the way I left. I never forgot. I tried so desperately to let go. I've been alone now for four years fighting with the ghosts and haunting images of that night. I never forgave myself for letting her in. My heart wanted her too much for me to say no. I would have rather killed myself than watch the one and only person I had ever loved be taken from me like that." Jordan sat back slightly away from Callie's touch with the tears still sliding down her face like a waterfall. She reached up wiping them away only to have more fall.

"One of the other detectives that I worked with caught him six months after Rachel's death. He received the death sentence for taking an officer's life. I testified for two days during his trial because I was subpoenaed. A year after the hearing a few strings were pulled moving him to the top of the death row list and he was killed by lethal injection. I heard about it, but I couldn't go back. No matter how much I wanted to watch him die, I couldn't do it. The trial just about killed me. Even with him dead and gone he still haunted me from his grave every night. It wasn't until this recent case that my emotions took over letting him haunt me during the day as well."

"I can't imagine what that felt like. I saw a picture of Rachel. She was beautiful. All of those women looked like her."

"Those women were pawns in the sick twisted mind game the killer was playing with me. You see, the guy that abducted you was Weston Garrison's cousin, Andrew Dexon. He was the man that kept Garrison hidden until the police finally found him.

"Andrew took everything out on me and came after me himself trying to make the memory of his cousin alive again. He chose girls that resembled Rachel and purposely killed them the same way, yet he added a few other details like the rape and beating to make them suffer since he knew I would have the case." Jordan's tears turned to anger.

"Callie, he intentionally went after you and tried to kill you with a dose of lethal injection poison. He was trying to make me watch you die just like he watched his cousin take his last few breaths. I don't know and probably never will know how I was able to find you and also kill him. I wouldn't be able to live with myself anymore if he had taken you, too. It's my job to protect and I've failed twice."

"No Jordan you didn't fail, I'm still here," Callie said placing her hand on Jordan's wet face.

The detective backed away and stood up next to the bed. She walked over to the bathroom entrance and put on the short gray silk robe that was hanging on the back of the door to cover her nude body. "Don't you see, Callie, I'll only hurt you. You may be okay this time, but can't you see it's not over? I let myself get involved with Rachel and it cost her, her life. Now look at me, I've let you slip right passed my guard, I can't do it. I just can't do this again."

"Jordan what are you saying? Listen to yourself, Jordan. Damn it, I'm okay can't you see me sitting here? You just made love to me, can't you see I'm alive. I lo..."

"No, don't say it, Callie. Please don't tell me you love me," Jordan said.

Callie put her feet down next to the bed and stood up. Walking over to Jordan, she pushed her up against the wall pressing their bodies together, their lips meeting passionately. Callie forced her tongue into Jordan's mouth, parting her lips aggressively.

Jordan nibbled as she sucked Callie's tongue softly.

Her hands were on Callie's firm butt, pulling her tightly against her thigh. Callie untied the silk robe dropping it to the floor. She began backing up slowly bringing Jordan with her until they met the bed once again. Callie fell back with the muscular detective on top of her.

Jordan moved her mouth down to Callie's breasts alternating back and forth between them, sucking the hard nipples as she ran her hand down Callie's firm stomach pausing between her legs. She felt the heat of her warm wet center as she slipped two fingers inside of the hot flesh.

"Oh God...Jordan, Oh!" Callie was washed away in ecstasy, moaning with pleasure as Jordan slipped in and out of her, deeper with each thrust.

Jordan couldn't stop herself from gently rubbing back and forth against Callie's right thigh that was between her legs. When Callie began slamming her hips against Jordan's hand riding the waves of orgasm Jordan lost her self control and let go squeezing Callie's thigh tightly between her legs until it was over.

"Ah...damn...I..." Jordan's speech was slurred as she tried to apologize for letting herself go without being touched by Callie.

"Hey, don't look so sad. That was beautiful. I loved watching you and feeling you against me. Don't ever be sorry for being intimate with me. You touch me in ways that I've never been touched before."

Jordan didn't quite register what Callie had just said. Her mind was still lost in the clouds of sexual bliss that hovered above them. They fell asleep together just as before with Callie in Jordan's arms and the black, silk bed sheets tangled around them.

A little before five a.m. Jordan woke before the alarm and turned it off. She dressed quickly, scribbling a small note for Callie on her way out in the event of her waking up alone. Jordan spent her usual hour in the gym lifting free weights, running on the treadmill, and using various cardio machines. She completely forgot about the sight of the naked woman upstairs in her bed. She returned to find the suite empty. At the bottom of her note was a message from Callie, *See you at the office. I had a wonderful night. Always, Callie.* Jordan never told Callie about the medical leave of absence or the suspension.

Jordan went on with her usual morning habits, taking a hot, steamy shower to wash away the memory of last night's events, and then went back to work on her case files. She returned a voicemail from her captain asking her to come into his office later that afternoon. She had a feeling she knew what it was about and began preparing herself for the briefing that would follow the returned voicemail.

The detective dressed casually professional in a pair of charcoal gray pants and a black polo shirt. She carried a small black gym bag at her side containing her issued hand gun, her badge, and the vindicating file she had on the Bay City Killer.

CHAPTER TWELVE

Jordan walked into the station and a few of the patrol officers smiled at her as she walked towards the elevator. None of them really knew her personally, her persona was too mysterious for most people, yet deep down they all wanted to be as cold hearted as she was on the job. There was no fictional story about her career; everyone knew she was the best of the best when it came to homicide investigation.

The Captain's office door was slightly ajar. She knocked softly as she pushed through the opening. She saw a somewhat older, salt and pepper haired man sitting in the leather chair to the right. He looked up from a small handful of papers on top of his briefcase and she noticed his marble gray eyes searching her face. They looked so similar to the eyes she never thought she'd see again.

"I've been expecting you," the man said.

The Captain waited until she was inside the office before he spoke. "Lieutenant, please close the door and have a seat next to Agent Doyle."

Jordan froze, blinking her eyes several times as the name and the unmistakable eyes registered in her mind. Swallowing the huge lump in her throat, she sat down as the Agent next to her extended his hand. She returned the gesture, shaking back firmly.

"Agent Doyle, this is Lieutenant Detective Jordan

Denali. Lieutenant, this is FBI Special Agent Glen Doyle," the captain said.

"Thank you, Captain Osborne, Lieutenant Denali, this is a confidential meeting. I've reviewed all of your case documentation, as well as your private personnel files here and also in Washington DC. I would like to offer you this Letter of Acceptance from the Federal Bureau of Investigation. If you chose to accept the letter, you will start Monday. This will leave you two days to conclude your ties here. Your flight arrangements have already been made," Agent Doyle said. His voice was deeper than she expected.

Jordan sat in silence trying not to move a muscle. She had no idea what to say. She wondered if this man even knew who she really was. That she was the one who got his daughter killed.

"Agent Doyle, with all due respect, I forgot all about applying for a position with the FBI. It's been well over four years. I'm not sure why…"

"Yes, Lieutenant, I'm aware of this. I know a lot about your life and your career."

"What makes the Bureau interested in me all of a sudden? I'm only a city level Homicide Detective," Jordan said.

"The Bureau doesn't care about your position at this level. What matters, is the way you handle it. You've been successful at tracking two serial killers on top of the many separate homicide investigations that you've been the lead detective on, not to mention your military career. The Bureau consists of many different levels of investigative experience. Your career stands out here in the civilian world, therefore, you're a top candidate." The older gentleman sat firmly in his chair with a very serious expression on his face.

Damn, Jordan, you've waited for this your whole career. What's wrong? Why now? It would be so easy to say yes. Don't throw it away. Jordan sat tightly composed in the leather chair next to the stiff agent. Her mind was lost, fighting battle after battle against her heart. She knew what had to be done. She was still confused as to why this man was sitting in her captain's office to begin with.

"Agent Doyle, may I please have a moment alone with Captain Osborne?"

As soon as the door was closed, she leaned forward in her chair with her hands resting against the edge of the desk balled up into fists. "Did you do this? Are you the one who called him?" Jordan's stiff attitude held itself as her voice raised only in her head.

"No, Jordan, he called me the day the story broke in the news. I answered a few questions, then he showed up here this morning. This was the first time I heard of this conversation. The only thing he said to me before you arrived was that he was here to speak with you about your application. I'm as confused about this as you are. I never knew that you applied to be a special agent. I damn sure don't want to lose you. He's right though. You're extraordinarily talented on the street. With everything you do being always by the book, you would damn sure make one hell of an agent, Lieutenant. You're exactly what they're looking for."

"I know," Jordan's voice faded off.

"What was that Jordan?"

"I'd like to continue my meeting with Agent Doyle privately in my office, if that is okay with you?" Jordan said.

"Sure. It's your life and your decision, Jordan," he said. "You're a huge asset to the civilian world. You're one in a hundred, Jordan. You give your life to your investigations. Whatever you choose, I know you'll make it your life to continue to be successful."

Jordan found the agent sitting in a chair outside of her office sipping a cup of coffee.

"Please come in, Agent Doyle," Jordan said waving him inside her office. She watched him sit stiffly in the chair across from her desk. Her hands were trembling in her lap as she sat in her desk chair. "What exactly would happen to me if I accepted the letter?" she asked.

"First of all, you should know Captain Osborne spoke highly of you this morning. You're probably the best second in command that he's ever had here. Anyway, you would arrive Sunday evening and Monday morning you would be taken to the main office for a briefing. From there, you begin your three week training session where you are taught everything you would ever need to know about the Bureau. At the end of your training, you would be sworn in and assigned to a field agent to work under for the following three weeks.

"After that you're given an apartment in the city to live in until you're assigned to a more permanent branch office, but you would only be there until the first Monday morning briefing. Then, you're sent to the Academy in Quantico, Virginia for one week of training in the NATU (New Agent Training Unit) and one week in the ITU (Investigative Training Unit). After that you come back to Washington and complete your last week at our Headquarters. Once all of your training is complete you begin your first assignment."

Jordan had a million questions running through her

mind, none of which pertained to the Bureau. "I do have one question for you. How much do you really know about me?"

"If you're asking whether or not I know of your involvement with my daughter, the answer is yes. I know everything, Jordan," he said.

"Then, with all due respect, I don't understand why you are here asking me to join the FBI."

"I will never forget the day my little girl called to tell me she was working on her first big case thanks to a detective named Jordan Denali. I heard the admiration in my daughter's voice and knew right away she was in love with you. I researched your entire life trying to figure out a way to pull her away from you. In doing so, I realized you were the best thing that had ever happened to her and there was no way I'd get her away from you to begin with. She was just like me and as stubborn as a mule. She didn't talk to me all that often, but when she did, she was always so happy. She told me once that you had applied to the Bureau and she planned to follow behind you after making detective with the police department. She said the two of you together would be the best pairing the FBI had ever seen," he said smiling slightly.

Jordan desperately tried not to let the tear in the corner of her eye slip out.

"When she died, I cursed myself for not stopping her from becoming an officer in the first place, but she gave her life doing what she loved to do. Jordan, I know what happened that morning. I've read that report a hundred times over the last four years. You weren't to blame. You followed protocol as you always do. Things happen in life that are extremely unfortunate sometimes," he paused.

"I looked for you at the funeral and was surprised to see you drop off the grid and pop back up in California. I've followed your career for the past four years and when I saw you in the news recently, I realized you'd finally come back from the dark hole you disappeared into. You're damn good at what you do and you took a chance on my daughter, teaching her how to be a detective when you didn't need to. I figured it was time I granted her wish and took a chance on you."

Jordan shook her head. "I should have never taken her with me that day. I should've never gotten close to her to begin with, but I couldn't say no. It was her dream to have us working together in the FBI." Jordan grinned. "I will never stop blaming myself for her death no matter what anyone says to me. I was there and I wasn't able to stop him."

"You stopped him this time, Jordan. Don't deliberately discard yourself. Rachel wouldn't want that. She adored you. If she's looking down on you right now from wherever she is, I'm sure she's telling you to make the right decision and move on with your life."

"I still love her and miss her every day. I think I probably always will, but you're right. She would want me to make the right decision for myself. Would you mind giving me a day or two?" Jordan asked.

"Here's my card. Let me know what you decide. You're plane leaves on Sunday morning," he said.

~

Jordan stood, glancing around her office before she proceeded down the hallway to the captain's office.

"I wanted to let you know I haven't made a decision.

I…"

"Have a seat, Lieutenant. Please Jordan, sit down," the captain said.

"Jordan, with your status here and current propositions, any field detective would jump on your opportunity. I can't say that I would, or could, ever fault you. It's not my place to disapprove of your actions. I can only control what goes on behind the walls of this division. Your future is most definitely your own responsibility. Chose what you believe would be best for you. Mistakes are sometimes harder to erase than they are to correct," he said. Deep down, he knew she would go. On the surface, he wished with everything he had that she would stay. Given the possibility to be an FBI Agent, he would've most definitely followed her right out the door himself.

Jordan couldn't believe the words her captain was saying. She could hear the faint sound of choking back tears as he spoke to her, not as her superior, but more like a father. It was definitely more reasonable than the ass chewing she was expecting from him. She beat out the suspension he planned for her, that itself was almost worth leaving behind.

"Sir, I…" The Captain cut her off in mid sentence.

"I don't really care to hear it, Denali. I have to get some things taken care of here before you decide to go. You will need to turn in your department issued gear and the Bay City Killer file. You can leave it all with Lance if you'd like. I know you'll leave without saying goodbye, that's just your manner. I'll take care of closing the case," he said.

Jordan held up the small black gym bag she brought with her. "Both of my guns, my badge, and my BP vest are in here. The file is in here as well." She set the bag on top of the wooden desk between them. "For the record, Captain, I never said I was going anywhere. This is the biggest decision of my life and I'm not taking it lightly. I will either see you Monday or I won't," she said.

~

Back at the extravagant hotel she was living in, Jordan paid the rental fee for another three months. Whether she accepted the letter or not, she wasn't ready to give up the beautiful penthouse suite she'd been living in for four years.

Jordan sat on the couch staring out of the large picture window overlooking the city. She could see the bay in the far off distance. Going back to Washington, DC was something she'd never thought possible. She made the disastrous trip back to finally say her goodbye to Rachel and in her mind that would be last time she'd ever see that city again. Now she was possibly returning there permanently in less than forty eight hours. *I hope you know what you're doing, Jordan.*

Jordan tried to file her thoughts of Callie deep in the back of her mind. The only way she could do this, take this position and move on with her career, was to be completely devoted to her work and her new training.

Instead of being overly excited, or even the least bit eager about the idea of starting a new federal career, Jordan felt lost, unsure if she was even capable of making a true decision. Her mind was telling her this is it, you've finally made it. Her heart was telling her that running away from a beautiful and charming woman was not one of the best things to do. She wasn't even sure if she was capable of having a relationship. Losing Rachel destroyed that side of her. *It would be so much easier to just go if I didn't have these goddamn heart aching feelings for her. I don't regret making love to her for one second, but I don't know if I can let myself fall in love again. It's not worth the heartache.*

~

Lance was called into the Captains office shortly after Jordan left the building. He was informed that Jordan was more than likely not returning to the San Francisco Police Department after being offered a position with the FBI. He was shocked. Part of him wanted to leave with her, the other part of him wanted to hate her for leaving.

After the captain dismissed him out of the office, he figured this was as good a time as any to go check on Callie. He knew she had returned to work and he hadn't seen her since his last visit to the hospital.

Callie was in a meeting so Lance waited in her office while Chloe went to let her know there was someone waiting to see her. Callie tried to keep it to a graceful walk instead of the full fledged sprint she had in mind as she walked down the hall towards her office. The smile on her face stretched from ear to ear as she opened the door.

The surprise took over both of them as she entered. Lance couldn't believe the smile on her face. Thinking it was because of him; he leaned forward and embraced her tightly. Callie was shocked to see Lance instead of Jordan standing in her office and now hugging her. She backed out of the embrace moving to her chair behind the desk.

"Lance, what brings you here?" she said with a confused look on her face.

"I wanted to see how you were doing, Doctor. I'm glad to see you're doing well."

"Yes, I'm fine. Thanks for the concern. How is Jordan? She must be sitting at her desk right now, agonizing over her paperwork as usual."

"Well, she's not exactly at her desk. But I didn't come here to gossip about Jordan anyway," he said.

"If she's not at her desk then where is she?"

"Her medical leave of absence was supposed to be through next week, and then her suspension was to follow..."

"But? Lance you're leaving something out. She never mentioned an LOA, but she also never mentioned a suspension either. Is she okay?" Callie was growing concerned. Jordan didn't say anything about not returning to work that morning.

"I believe she's fine. She's probably packing right now. Look, I don't want to talk about Jordan. I came up here to see how you were and ask you if you would like to have lunch with me sometime, or maybe dinner tonight even."

"What? Packing? Why would she be packing? Where is she going?" *Damn you, Jordan, don't run out on me now.*

"Uh, did you not just hear me ask you out, Dr. Marceau?" Lance said waiting for a response.

"I'm sorry, Lance. I just...I can't go anywhere right now. I'm too busy and I really don't want to hurt you. I'm actually seeing someone." *Or least I thought I was.*

"Oh, well that's okay. I can't say that I blame him. You're a very beautiful woman. If you ever want to just have a friendly casual lunch, you know where to find me," he sighed.

"Wait! Tell me what's going on with Jordan. Please, Lance, I have to know."

"I'm not sure what is happening yet. Captain Osborne said he was waiting until Monday to inform the department."

"Inform them of what exactly?"

"Jordan was accepted to the FBI this morning. If she takes their offer she leaves Sunday night for Washington, DC." Before Lance could finish his sentence, Callie shooed him out of her office closing the door behind him.

"Goddamn you, Jordan Denali, how could you do this to me?" The tears began slowly flowing out of her eyes and down her cheeks. "I thought I would have a chance to...damn it, Jordan. Damn you, damn you, Callie, for letting this happen to yourself."

Callie wiped her face with a tissue, realizing this was not the best place for a meltdown. She left her office without anyone noticing her leave an hour early.

~

Just as Jordan finally sat down on the couch with the glass of ice water that she'd opted for over the scotch, there was a loud knock on the door. *Who the hell could that be? Damn front desk and elevator attendants, I'm suppose to get a fucking call when I have a visitor. What kind of hotel is this?* Out of habit she quickly went into the bedroom to grab her service gun and noticed for the first time in four years she didn't have it anymore. *Fuck.* She decided against dealing with the wall safe in the living room where her personal gun was locked away.

She quietly went to the door and checked the peep hole before deciding whether or not to call security or just punch the asshole in the face. Callie was standing on the other side and she looked furiously pissed off. Jordan hesitated in opening the door.

"Callie?"

Callie pushed her way past Jordan and inside the foyer. She walked over to the living room with her back towards the detective, trying to hold back the tears threatening to fall.

"Don't say it, don't you dare ask me why I'm here. You were planning on leaving and never saying a word to me, not even goodbye. We made love for god's sake! Do you not have any compassion at all, or are you just a heartless bitch?" Callie sneered.

"Callie please, I don't know how to make you understand. I never meant…"

"You never meant to fuck me! Oh, I totally understand, damn you Jordan. Damn you for hurting me."

Jordan walked up to her wanting to touch her, hold her, take away the heartbreaking pain she was causing Callie to feel. *Damn it, Callie, I can't do this…I just can't.*

"Callie, please, it's not like that. I don't know what to do. I can't do this."

"What do you mean you can't do this? You had this all planned out and you never bothered to tell me you even applied for that job. This is just like you, Jordan, just like you. You fucking run from everything! I don't understand you. I thought maybe I had you figured out last night when you made love to me. I feel like it meant nothing to you. It obviously was nothing if you've forgotten about it already and were planning on leaving anyway."

Jordan moved towards her.

"Don't touch me! Don't you ever touch me again!"

"Callie, damn you, please listen to me."

"Why should I? I can't believe I had to find out from your partner that you were leaving for good in forty eight hours. You know this is more than just you not telling me about it or even telling me goodbye. Jordan, you should have told me you were thinking of doing this. You never once thought about my feelings or how our making love together would be affected by your decision to leave like this. I fucking have a heart and feelings too, damn you."

"Sit down, Callie. No I mean it, sit down, you need to hear this!" *Damn you, Lance, you stupid ass!*

Callie sat down on the couch and Jordan walked over to the adjacent loveseat.

"I didn't just think of doing this two days ago, Callie." She put her hand up when Callie tried to say something. "Please let me talk. I have every right to speak too. You've been telling me off since you walked in the door.

"Like I said, I didn't just do this. I applied for a position with the FBI over four years ago. Rachel talked me in to it when we first got together. It was her dream to work there together as a team one day. I had forgotten all about until this morning when I went in for my suspension meeting with Captain Osborne and Rachel's father was sitting in the captain's office with an acceptance letter. I didn't realize he was even in the FBI. She only said he worked for the government and she didn't talk to him much. I'm sorry, Callie. I never meant to hurt you."

"Jordan, you could have talked to me. I'm not stupid.

I know you're choosing this and running away. The FBI is your escape. Have you even just once thought about how it will affect you, living in DC again? Or maybe how it will affect me and my feelings for you? All you think about is yourself, Jordan. You know, this isn't going to bring her back, no matter how hard you try, you can never bring her back, Jordan. She's gone. You have to move on with your life."

"Callie, this has nothing to do with Rachel. Please listen to me, I swear it doesn't. This is the second time today I've been told that she's gone and I need to move on with my life. Agent Doyle said the same thing to me this morning. Only he wants me to move on in his direction and you want me to move on by staying here," Jordan said shakily.

She was confused. Callie was right. She wanted to run like hell in the opposite direction. She was so tired of running from the pain and ghosts that haunted her dreams. After losing Rachel, she swore she'd never love again, and then Callie broke her. She crossed the line and Jordan couldn't stop her. Leaving was a way out, a way to stop the agonizing feelings since she finally let her guard down. In Jordan's mind, all she ever did was hurt everyone. She knew it was love that she was feeling and she was scared to death.

"Jordan, I'm not Rachel, and I'm not dead. You have to look at me, please, it's over. Can't you see you've won, Jordan. I'm alive and he's dead. He can't come after you anymore. You saved my life. It's okay for you to be with me. You have to trust me, please. I don't know how to let you go," Callie said wiping tears from her eyes.

Jordan knew deep down she wanted to be with Callie, but thinking of all of the horrendous events of the past few months felt all too familiar. Her heart was scared. How many times would she have to go through those events? The ghosts still haunted her in the night. How long would that continue? Would the ghosts ever go away? Could she ever give herself whole heartedly to this woman?

Callie could see the emotional roller coaster Jordan was on. She stood up and walked over to Jordan. Sitting next to her, she put her arms around Jordan, pulling her close.

"Jordan, I'm right here. I will never ever walk away from you. I care for you deeply. I don't want you to go. I don't want you to run from me. I promise I'll never hurt you. I want to help you fight off the ghosts of your past. I want to see the future with you. You saved my life and you finally beat everything that was against you. It's okay to stop running now. Jordan, I love you. I've loved you since the moment I first saw you."

Jordan looked into green eyes that were almost clear from all of the crying, as she pressed her moist lips against Callie's. She slipped her arms around Callie's waist as one of Callie's hands moved to Jordan's neck with her thumb massaging her ear. Callie's other hand was between Jordan's chest and shoulder with Callie's fingers lying against her collarbone.

Jordan backed away slightly, her face bending down towards Callie's shoulder as her lips met Callie's neck placing a few gentle kisses against the tender, warm skin before moving her lips to Callie's ear.

"Come on," Jordan growled as she stood up pulling Callie with her.

They stopped next to the king sized bed. Callie pulled the dark colored polo shirt Jordan was wearing over her head and unbuttoned the dress slacks around her waist. Their lips meeting fiercely as Jordan followed Callie's lead, helping her out of her clothes as well.

Naked, they pressed against each other. Callie stepped back, lying down between the smooth sheets. Jordan moved with her, laying her own body on top of Callie's between her legs, kissing Callie again as their bodies met.

Jordan moved her mouth away from Callie's lips, breaking the kiss long enough to suck lightly on a tense nipple as her hand ran down the side and across the firm stomach muscles of Callie's slender body. Callie rolled Jordan over to her back and sat up straddling Jordan's waist as she caressed her breasts teasing the pink nipples between her fingers and thumbs. She moved back down on top of Jordan, sliding down between her legs, licking a path down both thighs with her tongue lazily leading to her center.

"Ah, God touch me, Callie, please." Jordan ran her hands through Callie's hair as it fell against her thighs.

Callie slid her tongue slowly around the wet mound, then deep inside of Jordan as she bucked with pleasure. Jordan could barely hold on, reaching the edge before she could stop herself. She exploded as Callie continued licking softly, avoiding her throbbing clit. She wanted more. Jordan felt her body stiffen up again while the throbbing increased with every touch of Callie's tongue.

The heightened sensitivity caused Jordan to shutter as Callie sucked gently on her until Jordan could no longer hold on. She moaned loudly as her body released itself to Callie.

"You taste almost as good as you look, did you know that?" Callie teased kissing Jordan's thighs.

Jordan could hardly catch her breath. "You look good down there," Jordan teased back.

Callie crawled back up Jordan's body. Their lips met uncontrollably this time, holding nothing back. Jordan forcefully rolled Callie over onto her back sliding down between her parted legs. Her hands tenderly massaged Callie's breasts, squeezing the nipples and running her fingers across them just as Callie had done to her.

"I want you, Jordan. I want you so bad, I can't take it anymore. Touch me!"

Jordan ran her hands along Callie's sides and then over her thighs as her tongue began to lick and suck her, alternating back and forth. Callie's hands went from tearing at the sheets to tugging affectionately on Jordan's hair.

"Ah...ah!" Callie was holding on for dear life to Jordan's hands that intertwined with hers as her body soared to the top of the most excruciatingly powerful orgasm she had ever felt. Several small crests followed to intensify the ecstasy she was feeling. Jordan moved back to Callie's side as Callie rolled over to kiss her lips delicately.

"I love you, Jordan," Callie whispered.

Jordan knew she felt the same. She smiled softly and pulled Callie's head down to her shoulder wrapping her arms around her. She laid there breathing in the sweet scent of Callie's hair, and listening to her breathing slow down as she fell asleep. *God, if I've ever needed you, now would be the time for you to answer me back. Please forgive me if I don't know what to do. I'm lost in her. My heart is torn from the thoughts in my head and the feelings in my body. I can't hurt her anymore. Please don't let me hurt her anymore. I...I love her, god I love her so much and I'm so scared. It's been so long since I've loved. I swore I would never love another. God, please, I'm begging you to help me. Help me do what's right. It's so hard, the darkness of my past colliding with the brightness of Callie and my future. It's killing me. It's time for it to stop. It's time for me to let go.*

~

The alarm went off before dawn as usual. Jordan reached for the alarm realizing Callie was asleep half on top of her. By the time Jordan wiggled out from under Callie, stopped to brush the hair away and kiss her forehead, Callie woke up.

"Uh, where are you going? The sun isn't even up yet." Callie was squinting her eyes, trying not to let in the light from the bathroom.

"Are you going to answer me, Jordan? Where are you going this early?"

"Callie, you know I go to the gym at the same time every day. It's okay. I'll be back in an hour. Go back to sleep. When I get back we can shower together and go get some breakfast, if you're hungry." Jordan bent down and put her arms around Callie as she kissed her lips lightly, forcing her tongue between them. "I'll be back soon, I promise."

Callie was fast asleep by the time Jordan was dressed for the gym. She went down the elevator and into the large room full of equipment. There was never anyone there this early. Jordan purposely set it up that way since the gym wasn't supposed to open until seven. She was the Penthouse guest and had been for just over four years. She was definitely paying enough to have a private key card to the gym so she could make up her own hours.

Jordan worked through her usual gym routine then swam about fifteen laps before returning to her suite to find Callie still sleeping and snoring softly. She looked like an angel lying in Jordan's bed. Her naturally tanned skin and long dark hair blended in with the black silk sheets. Jordan bent down running her fingers through Callie's hair gracefully, then down her back. *God, just looking at her makes me weak in the knees. Touching her makes me drown in my own desire for her. She has such a powerful control over me. It's like I'm her possession, whether I want to be or not. Of course I want to be. Look at her. She's the most beautiful, passionate person I have ever seen. God, I've fallen for her so fast. I can't explain the way she makes me feel. I know I love her.*

Callie awoke feeling Jordan's hands running over her body.

"There you are. I was wondering when you'd return. I missed you," Callie said stretching and sitting up to hug Jordan. She backed away quickly. "Gross! You're sweaty, and…" She sniffed the air. "You stink," She laughed as Jordan pulled her close and planted a wet kiss on Callie's mouth.

"It takes a lot to look like this. I'll gladly give up the gym and grow massive love handles if that's what you want," Jordan taunted.

"No, don't you dare. I love your body. You're sexy as hell," Callie said.

"Come on, if I smell so bad, and look as sweaty and as sticky as I feel, then I definitely need a shower. Will you do me the honor of joining me?"

"Well, let's see, hmm…yes of course I'll join you." Callie smiled.

Both women stepped into the hot, steamy waterfall behind the glass door. They took turns soaping, shampooing and rinsing each other. Jordan pulled Callie into the water with her, their lips meeting with a fiery hunger. Jordan pushed Callie against the tiled wall and ran her hand down the front of Callie's body, stopping with her fingers massaging the already swollen mound of flesh between her legs.

Callie moaned with pleasure as Jordan slipped two fingers inside of her. Jordan held Callie tight against her body as she slid her fingers in and out, rhythmically causing Callie's hips to rock against her with each thrust.

"You feel so good," Callie said breathlessly.

Jordan kissed her passionately, sucking and nibbling her lips. Callie tightened around her fingers, moaning into her mouth. She wrapped her arms firmly around Jordan holding on for dear life as her body lost control.

Jordan smiled and leaned back just enough to look into her eyes, promising not to let go of the shivering woman in case she forgot she was standing.

"I think I can't feel my legs or my feet. Oh, Jordan, what did you do to me? You make me feel so alive, like I'm in another world when you touch me."

"I know, you make me feel the same way," Jordan said.

They both got out of the shower, quickly toweling off in the cool air. Callie put her hands on Jordan's shoulders, running them down her back. Jordan turned around to face her.

"God, I want you, but we better not start this again. I'm starving. If I don't eat real food I may pass out," Jordan said leaning forward. She kissed Callie's lips softly then pulled away. "Come on, I think I may have something here that'll fit you. We're pretty close in size."

"I don't think I planned ahead," Callie laughed. When she showed up at Jordan's door on Friday night unannounced, an overnight bag wasn't exactly on her mind.

"You can look for a shirt in there." Jordan said pointing to the walk-in closet. "Most of it is dress shirts and polo's, I have a few tee shirts also, take your pick."

Jordan dressed in a pair of light colored jeans and a dark blue polo shirt. She sat on the bed and put her black leather shoes on. Callie came out of the closet wearing her jeans from the night before that were still clean and a tight fitting, low-cut, black shirt that she'd found in the back of the closet.

"Wow, you look…where did that shirt come from? I don't think I've ever seen it. It looks marvelous on you though."

"It still had the tag on it. I must say you've got expensive, yet, amazing taste when it comes to clothes. It figures all of your suits are Armani, and your blouses are all Gucci. I thought I spent a lot of money on clothes, but damn, Jordan. Not to mention the fact that you live in the penthouse of a hotel. I won't bother to ask how or why," Callie said.

Jordan laughed, wondering where that shirt had come from. It must have been an accidental impulse buy because it was definitely Callie's style. She couldn't help her infatuation with top of the line clothing and she chose to live in one of the most expensive hotels in town because of her obsession for high class and the intimidating threat of settling down somewhere.

"It's a fetish of mine, I guess. I collect clothing. I've always had a thing for luxury, and you're absolutely correct, it is an expensive hobby."

"I noticed you were wearing a Rolex watch the first time I saw you. I had to smile, thinking in the back of my mind, this woman is not only beautiful, she takes pride in the way she looks. You flaunt yourself and you don't even know it. It's an adorable feature of yours."

"Well, I'm not the only one with an expensive taste in clothing. I guess I just take it further than you," Jordan said smiling.

Callie zipped up her black ankle boots and turned towards Jordan.

"Your paycheck must be a hell of a lot bigger than mine," Callie said smiling back.

"I guess there is still a lot we need to talk about," Jordan said.

"I wish you would stop hiding things from me, Jordan."

Jordan sighed and sat down on the corner of the bed. "I don't like to talk about my life."

"You don't like to talk about anything," Callie said sitting down next to her.

Jordan grinned. "You're right. It's complicated. I'm sort of estranged from my family. My parents and little brother were killed in a plane crash when I was fifteen. My father was an amazing pilot and worked in the R&D department of an aeronautical company. The president of the company lent him a prototype plane to fly all of us up to Canada on vacation. I got sick with the stomach flu so I didn't go with them. The plane crashed in the middle of the flight due to a flaw in the hydraulic assembly for the wing flaps that was supposedly fixed."

"Oh my God, Jordan. I'm so sorry."

"Thanks. It's been a long time. Anyway, my dad was

the one who pointed out the flaw and it was going to cost the company millions of dollars to fix the flaw in the planes that were already being built and more than a year to redesign the system. My father was told that it had been fixed and they even had a test flight that went fine. The problem was that it was never fixed. They sort of put a band-aid on the problem for the test flight without him knowing and it worked. So, they put the same band-aid on the first planes to roll off the assembly line and my father was the first to fly one of them."

"Wow."

"My father's best friend worked for the company too and was able to copy all of my father's notes and research before they deleted everything. He turned it over to the authorities and that was enough to prove them guilty of negligent homicide for all three of my family members. My grandmother sued the company for wrongful death and won a very large sum of money that was set up in a trust fund for me. I graduated high school and joined the Marine Corps, so I missed all of the trials and everything. I started getting the quarterly payouts when I turned thirty. I had no idea what to do with all of the money so I just started putting it in the bank. Rachel knew about my family, but not about the trust fund. I was embarrassed about it, I guess. I didn't want the money. It was blood money to me," Jordan sighed.

"When Rachel died I gave up on everything and moved across the country. That's when I started spending my money. I blew thousands of dollars on nothing at first. I was so confused. I didn't know how to lose her, too, after losing my family. Finally, I realized how much I missed being a cop and went to the captain to ask for a job and here I am."

"You're a woman of mystery, Jordan. I don't really know what to say. You don't have to be embarrassed about having money no matter how you got it. Obviously, you know money isn't everything. What I don't understand is how you're estranged from your family."

"My grandmother doesn't agree with my lifestyle. She thinks I should marry a man and live in a big house with a pile of kids. If she could stop my payouts she would, but I'm an adult and she has no control over it. She actually tried to take it all when I was in Iraq and my lawyer had to go to court for me against her. She lives and breathes the bible and it's really sad. It's also ironic how when her son died, she all of a sudden tucked the bible away and became this highly educated woman that spent every waking minute fighting for her son and his family's rights. Then, once everything was over, the bible came back out of the drawer. When I came home from Iraq and was discharged, she tried to comfort me and was supposedly so thankful I was alive. I thought maybe we could be a family again. I told her I was a lesbian and all hell broke loose."

"That's sad. I'm sorry."

"Don't be. I've moved on with my life," Jordan said looking at her.

"What did you do in the Marines?"

"Infantry. I was deployed to Iraq. The president had come over for a visit with the troops and a group of Iraqi soldiers tried to assassinate him. My convoy was deployed for protection as they rushed to get the president out of the country. We were ambushed a few miles outside of Bagdad. I was shot here," Jordan said lifting her shirt to show the tiny inch wide scar. "The bullet came out back here." She turned around showing the larger scar on her back.

"I noticed the scars." Callie smiled, remembering her hands on Jordan's body.

"One of our crew members died and the three of us that survived were imprisoned for three weeks in an abandoned building in the middle of the city. I managed to kill one of the guards and we escaped. Our unit found us a few days later. I came home severely injured and received a bunch of medals. That was a long time ago."

"You're full of surprises."

Jordan smiled. "Does all of this bother you?"

"What?"

"Any of it? The hotel, the expensive clothes, the trust fund? My life?"

"No, I don't care how or where you get your money from or even the fact that you have money. It's a little shocking, I'll be honest, but I don't care about money or your lifestyle. I care about you," Callie said.

Jordan grabbed Callie's hand, interlacing their fingers.

" Have you decided what you're going to do?" Callie said squeezing her hand and changing the subject.

"About the FBI?"

"Yes."

Jordan sighed running a hand through her hair. "I thought I knew until I woke up in the middle of the night," she said.

"I can't say goodbye to you. Despite your secrets and enigmatic behavior, I love you, Jordan."

Jordan pulled Callie tightly into her arms. "I know. Callie, I..."

"I know how you feel. You don't have to say it. I know it's hard for you to say. I know because I can feel it when you look at me and when you touch me and I hear it when you say my name."

Callie stepped forward pressing her lips against Jordan's. Their tongues glided as though they had known each other forever. Callie's arms moved around Jordan's neck, playing in the back of her hair. Jordan wrapped her arms tightly around Callie's waist, running her hands up and down her back as the kiss deepened. Jordan backed away to catch her breath with her arms still loosely around Callie's waist.

"Dr. Marceau, we better stop this. I can hardly control myself. I'm so wrapped up in you. I'm liable to let myself go and forget to tell you I'm staying here."

"What do you mean you're staying here?"

"I mean I'm not going to DC. I realized I'm right where I need to be and want to be. I...I love you, Callie."

Callie pulled Jordan against her for another searing kiss. Tugging Jordan's shirt loose from her jeans, she ran her hands against the warm, soft skin.

"If you don't stop that, we're going to miss breakfast," Jordan said between kisses.

"Would that be a bad thing, Lieutenant?" Callie said with a conniving smile and a wink as she kissed her again.

About the Author

Austen spends her days working in the corporate world and her nights bringing her stories to life. She's an avid reader and claims to have too many favorite authors to narrow it down to one. She blames her love of books on the countless hours she has spent flying all over the country and sleeping in stuffy hotel rooms.

You can contact Austen at austenthorne@gmail.com and like her fan page on facebook.com/austenthorne

Go to www.tri-pub.com to get information about Triplicity Publishing or to submit your own manuscript.

Other Titles Available From Triplicity Publishing

Falling Snow by Graysen Morgen. Dr. Cason Macauley, a high-speed trauma surgeon from Denver meets Adler Troy, a professional snowboarder and sparks fly. The last thing Cason wants is a relationship and Adler doesn't realize what's right in front of her until it's gone, but will it be too late? (978-1477410752)

Fate vs. Destiny by Graysen Morgen. Logan Greer devotes her life to investigating plane crashes for the National Transportation Safety Board. Brooke McCabe is an investigator with the Federal Aviation Association who literally flies by the seat of her pants. When Logan gets tangled in head games with both women will she choose fate or destiny? (978-1477410691)

Just Me by Graysen Morgen. Wild child Ian Wiley has to grow up and take the reins of the hundred year old family business when tragedy strikes. Cassidy Harland is a little surprised that she came within an inch of picking up a gorgeous stranger in a bar and is shocked to find out that stranger is the new head of her company. (978-1477410745)

Love Loss Revenge by Graysen Morgen. Rian Casey is an FBI Agent working the biggest case of her career and madly in love with her girlfriend. Her world is turned upside when tragedy strikes. Heartbroken, she tries to rebuild her life. When she discovers the truth behind what really happened that awful night she decides justice isn't good enough, and vows revenge on everyone involved. (978-0988619609)

Natural Instinct by Graysen Morgen. Chandler Scott is a Marine Biologist who keeps her private life private. Corey Joslen is intrigued by Chandler from the moment she meets her. Chandler is forced to finally open her life up to Corey. It backfires in Corey's face and sends her running. Will either woman learn to trust her natural instinct? (978-1477410714)

Secluded Heart by Graysen Morgen. Chase Leery is an overworked cardiac surgeon with a group of best friends that have an opinion and a reason for everything. When she meets a new artist named Remy Sheridan at her best friend's art gallery she is captivated by the reclusive woman. When Chase finds out why Remy is so sheltered will she put her career on the line to help her or is it too difficult to love someone with a secluded heart? (978-1477410677)

In Love, at War by Graysen Morgen. Charley Hayes is in the Army Air Force and stationed at Ford Island in Pearl Harbor. She is the commanding officer of her own female-only service squadron and doing the one thing she loves most, repairing airplanes. Life is good for Charley, until the day she finds herself falling in love while fighting for her life as her country is thrown haphazardly into World War II. Can she survive being in love and at war? (978-0988619616)

Fast Pitch by Graysen Morgen. Graham Cahill is a senior in college and the catcher and captain of the softball team. Despite being an all-star pitcher, Bailey Michaels is young and arrogant. Graham and Bailey are forced to get to know each other off the field in order to learn to work together on the field. Will the extra time pay off or will it drive a nail through the team? (978-0988619623)

Submerged by Graysen Morgen. Assistant District Attorney Layne Carmichael had no idea that the sexy woman she took home from a local bar for a one night stand would turn out to be someone she would be prosecuting months later. Scooter is a Naval Officer on a submarine who changes women like she changes uniforms. When she is accused of a heinous crime she is shocked to see her latest conquest sitting across from her as the prosecuting attorney. (978-1477410653)

Other Titles Coming Soon From Triplicity Publishing

Igniting Temptation by Sydney Canyon. Mackenzie Trotter is the Head of Pediatrics at the local hospital. Her life takes a rather unexpected turn when she meets a flirtatious, beautiful fire fighter. Both women soon discover it doesn't take much to ignite temptation.